COME BACK, GEORDIE

When the world rejoiced in getting to know Geordie MacTaggart, he was a young lad triumphing in the Olympic Games. Now he comes back to us, married to the Jean who inspired him to his victory and the father of Charlie, a teenage boy with all the troubles of his kind —and all their virtues.

God-like Geordie, hero, gamekeeper, strict and no nonsense father. A natural for starting a son's revolt. Fortunately our old friend, Geordie's patron, the Laird of Drumfechan is still very much in the picture, and with his daft wisdom sees the cause of the trouble and conspires for its cure.

Maggie was no Jean—a monstrous hulk of a girl and Charlie's enemy to the death. But if Geordie had been able to make his puny self into the world's great shot putter, Maggie, too, could work miracles—and did.

COME BACK, GEORDIE

GEORDIE

by

DAVID WALKER

COLLINS
ST JAMES'S PLACE, LONDON
1966

THERE ARE NO REAL PEOPLE IN THIS
BOOK; AND THE OLYMPIC GAMES HAVE
NOT YET TAKEN PLACE IN MONTREAL

To Giles,
Barclay, David, and Julian

© DAVID WALKER, 1966
PRINTED IN GREAT BRITAIN
COLLINS CLEAR-TYPE PRESS
LONDON AND GLASGOW

BOOK ONE

★ I ★

Down at the river an oyster-catcher whistled. Across the lea a pair of peewits wheeled and dived, and they were crying. Here Geordie MacTaggart and Charlie MacTaggart did not speak.

A few sounds here were Geordie's grunts, the thudding of the maul, the prideful squawk of a pullet after laying. It was June at Drumfechan, a rare fine morning in that Highland place, peaceful with the sunshine and the nesting and a world so green. The world around had a peaceful look.

"That's the posts done," Geordie said. "The wire'll not take long." They were making a fenced run for the Laird's new pullets; or Geordie was making it with conscripted labour.

Charlie held the coil of wire as he was bidden, scowling. His father stapled the poultry fence to the wall of the henhouse. Then they started round the posts. "Tighter," Geordie said.

"Yoo-Hoo!" A call came owl-like from the woods behind them. The Laird's *Yoo-Hoos* could mean different things—that the Laird was only announcing his presence; that the Laird was in the mood for a chat; that the Laird was excited about some news; that the Laird was in a warlike condition. It all depended on the length and tone and pitch of Yoos

and Hoos. Geordie had long ago learned to melt
away from the wrong combinations. But this one was
all right. "George! Where is the fella?"

"Here, sir," Geordie called. He went on hammering, and Charlie stopped scowling. "*Top o' the
mornin'*," he said to himself.

Soon the Laird of Drumfechan came down the
stone dike steps and across to them. As usual he
wore his old kilt which was in shreds at the bottom
and drooped down the back of his spindly legs and
was faded to the colour of tired rope. "Good morning,
George. Top o' the mornin', Charles. A new fox-
proof, even wolf-proof refuge for the débutantes, I
see." The Laird chuckled at his own bad joke, and
so did Charlie. "Are they laying yet?"

"Just getting started," Geordie said. He hoped the
Laird would not stay too long, because it was Saturday,
and he wanted to finish the job by dinner-time.

"A fine day like this, Charles old boy, you should
be tempting the wily trout, not building hen-runs with
your father."

No comment to that, and the Laird's beady eyes
darted from one MacTaggart to the other. "Talking
of fishes," he said, "or the lack of—I hear work's
going to start on the dam next month. City riff-raff
types—they'll corrupt the glen, you mark my words.
And the salmon will be ruined. Fish ladders, bah,
George, don't you agree?"

"Yessir," Geordie said. The Laird was talking
about the new power scheme which would raise the
level of Drumfechan Loch, and he was in full agreement with the Laird, but he wanted to get on with the
Laird's work. He hammered a staple.

"Talking of salmon again—if I'm to be back in time for your mother's, your grannie's excellent soufflé, I must be on my way. Left my glasses at Egypt's Camp, old idiot, last evening—a fine night fortunately."

"Does the Laird mean his specs?" Charlie said.

"No, no, boy—my snoopers."

"It's a fair long road to Egypt's Camp. If the Laird kens the place where the glasses are lying, mebbe Charlie could run for them."

"Oh, would you, Charles, what a capital notion." The Laird explained where his snoopers were lying at Egypt's Camp, the tree plantation. "And Charles! Sling them round your neck for optimum safety."

"Right, sir," Charlie said. He turned and ran for the glasses, ran from the work that was a punishment.

They watched him cross the park. "Fleet as the springbok," said the Laird. "You ever see a stride like that?" Charlie's legs were long and his stride was long. You felt that he was floating, flying in rubber-cleated boots and knickerbockers of Drumfechan tweed and the green jersey his mother had knitted for him. Now he was climbing the side of the glen, up the path through young bracken and hill birches. "Phenomenal," said the Laird. "Another future champion in the family, eh, George?"

"Last year he did the mile in four fifty-two, and him just fourteen. This time he wouldn't even enter —says running is running, but races is daft."

"H'm," said the Laird. "Like his father, if I remember aright."

Geordie hammered, and the Laird held the wire for him. They made quick work of it. Then Geordie filled in a trench round the foot of the fence, which was buried against marauders. And that was that job done.

"How does Charles seem these days?" the Laird asked casually.

"He's not just like himself," Geordie said. "Not lately. He was aye up to mischief, but cheery mischief, no harm to it. . . ."

"An excellent amusing boy, a credit to you, George. What's gone amiss?"

"Well, sir, it's this way . . ." Geordie had been thinking he might have a talk with the Laird about Charlie. The Laird had daft notions and did daft things, but about other folks' troubles he could be wise as a serpent in the Bible. So now, while they sat on an old stump in sunshine, he told the Laird his worries. Charlie was like a different boy. Charlie wouldn't give time to his lessons. Charlie would be rude to his mum, and Jean would get vexed, and there would be a blow-up. Charlie wouldn't be outside where a boy should be after lessons on a summer evening. Charlie would be sprawled on his bed, just reading, reading. "And the books, stuff I wouldn't want Jean to be after reading."

"Would you be after reading the stuff yourself?" asked the Laird.

Geordie smiled at the Laird's sly dig. "I might take a wee dip into them whiles. But I'm not a laddie just fifteen past, I'm forty-two."

"Almost sinless at forty-two, I'll wager," said the Laird. "At seventy my burden of sin is not short of colossal." He shook his scrawny shoulders, perhaps about sin's burden. "Continue, George."

Geordie continued that there was unkindness to

Charlie's mischief lately, like when he took Maggie Oliphant's panty bloomers from the washing line and painted her name wrong on them and stuffed them bulging full of straw and hung them from a bough outside the poor lassie's cottage.

The Laird frowned. "Yes," he said. "In the circs, unkind. But remember, George, that fifteen is not the age of kindness. Your own mischief, which was plenty, was never of the unkind variety. But like father like son is only part true. We must add the genes of the fiery Jean, angel of kindness though she is."

The Laird laughed at himself again, and then he said carefully and slowly, not like his usual rat-tat-tat: "I never had children of my own, but I think a father tends to see his son as himself and through himself, through the himself that he remembers imperfectly at that age."

"That's right, sir," Geordie said.

"Now at fifteen life was simple for you. At fifteen you already had a single gigantic purpose." The Laird meant that at fifteen Geordie was training on the long hard road to be six foot five and twenty stone and to win the Olympic Shot-putt.

". . . And then responsibility came to you at your father's early death. Most unfortunate, but it steadies a boy in the difficult years. Could you try giving Charles some responsibility?"

"I did, sir," Geordie said. He had had a bright idea that if he gave Charlie the vermin traps to look after, he would be running all over the hill to get in training and burn up his energy to keep him out of mischief or out of the house on the long summer evenings, and a useful job to do, and be paid a bit for it. It worked fine for a couple of weeks, and Charlie took a fair catch of stoats and weasels; and then last night instead of doing his Friday rounds, Charlie got on to the bike and rode off to Drumfechan village without so much as a word or an excuse. Geordie saw him go. So Geordie himself had to make the long walk to set the traps before the week-end. He paused. This was what he was leading up to, not to tell tales on Charlie, but because the Laird's opinion might be a help.

"Yes, George?" said the Laird, all ears and wide moustaches.

"The traps were sprung, every one, and nothing taken. Charlie had never set them the last time. So I says to him—he wasn't home till the back of ten, and no reason given, I says: *What's the meaning of it?* And he says, cheeky-like, he said: *I thought I'd give the poor craters a few days off.* So I says: *But, Charlie, you ken fine the vermin must be kept down.* And he says, getting vexed: *Haven't they as much right to live as you?*"

"Oh, I say," said the Laird. "That's a tricky one, age-old question, unanswerable in moral terms, simple as pie by jungle law."

"How could a keeper be letting the vairmin . . . ?"

"Yes yes, George, of course."

"Well then, he went to his room and brought down a book, some story he's been reading, and he said: *You listen, Dad, just listen to what this chap wrote*: and he read: '*It is a far worse crime to murder a dumb animal than to rape a willing wumman,*' or it was words to that . . ."

But the Laird had fallen off the tree-stump. He

cackled and heaved and wheezed, and tears ran down his hollow cheeks, and then the Laird choked and went purple which was worrying for a minute too, although Geordie was offended by the Laird's unseemly mirth. After a while his employer wiped eyes and straightened kilt on the good green grass, and he said: "Sorry, George, an unwilling surrender."

Geordie's hammering had kept the hens subdued, but now scratching and impatient clucking sounded in there. "The pullets are wanting out," he said, and went to open the slide door to the run. They came through in a rush to pluck at tender grass.

"Rhode Island Reds," the Laird said. "The same amiable thoroughbred fowls since time began, or I can remember. Now, if we were efficient, George . . ." And he rambled on about sex-linked crosses that could be distinguished at hatching time, and antibiotics to the cockerels to hurry them on for broilers, and change the hen flock every year. Efficiency was one of the Laird's pet subjects.

"I don't see the use of it," Geordie said. "We just need eggs and cockerels for the Laird's table, and we need second-year clockers for to raise the pheasant chicks. And that's what we have. So that's efficient."

"Yes, George. Efficiency a trifle out of date. What I mean, George, is that the world has changed. The world gallops faster and faster and madder and madder every day. But life in this glen has hardly changed at all, not in your day, hardly even in mine except for a few machines."

"There's television," Geordie said.

"True. We can sit at home and look through the telly at a daft world you and I don't begin to belong to. By the way, did you see Wyatt Earp, terrific this time, wasn't he? But what about an intelligent boy nowadays? Which is the world he begins to belong to, the backwater where he lives, or the real big world out there?"

"I never lived in a city," Geordie said. "I never lived even in a village."

"No," said the Laird. "Always in a country place that belongs to you and you to it. But young Charles . . ." The Laird didn't finish.

"He'll not stay here," Geordie said. "Jean and I ken that fine. With the brains he has, to be a keeper and stalker wouldn't be right. It would be a waste of the intelligence."

"Perhaps," said the Laird. "But it won't be a waste that he has grown up with parents he can respect. That will go with him. I think you forget how much that boy looks up to you."

"And what heed does he pay when I ask him to give attention to his lessons? Is that looking up?"

"Don't worry, George," the Laird said in a kindly way. "It'll be all right, you mark my words. Just don't expect too much of him. Is Charles still keen on forestry?"

"No," Geordie said. "That was last year, that idea."

"Ah, here he comes." The Laird stood up with a creaking of joints to watch Charlie run to them. He came back the way he had gone, down the path through hill birches and bracken, and across the park. Charles MacTaggart might make a great distance runner one day, but now he said that races were daft. His face was a little flushed, and the whites of his eyes as white as could be, and his hair a black Scotsman's curly black. His chest rose and fell, and his breathing slowed. He was a grand piper too, with a piper's lungs, but now he wouldn't play the pipes. Stop it, Geordie told himself. The old Laird is right. He's a grand laddie with the growing pains.

Charlie pulled the binoculars from inside his jersey neck. "They were on the stump just where you said, sir."

"Thanks a million, Charles. See anything of interest?"

"I saw two roedeer in the birks, a doe and a wee one."

"Not near the young plantation?"

"No, sir," Charles said. But the flicker of his eyes told Geordie that he lied to save the roedeer from his father's rifle.

"Graceful creatures," the Laird said, "but a perfect menace to young trees. Nature's balance, how to preserve what we upset. Now there's a thorny problem."

"We had an essay to write on that."

"Did you, though, Charles? A fascinatin' subject."

"I have it at home, if the Laird would like . . ."

"You bet I would."

Now Geordie took the heavy maul, and Charlie the other tools, and they walked with the Laird. Geordie had a small thought—it was jealousy, he knew—that Charlie would tell the Laird about his essay and would show it to him and listen to the Laird's ideas, but never a word about it to his own father, whose job was to be a gamekeeper, a keeper of nature's balance. He thinks I'm a muckle thick-headed lump with set ideas, Geordie thought. That's what I am too.

"I'll just get the essay," Charlie said. He ran again, tools clanking, and went up the steps in the grey stone dike, down through the woods to home.

"As I was trying to say, George, these are difficult times to be growing up, much harder than mine or even yours."

But Geordie could not quite see that. It seemed to him . . . "Why, sir?" he said.

"Because they have so much more, and they know so much more. Yet we rebelled against what we knew. They rebel against things too big to know."

"That's beyond me," Geordie said.

"Same here," said the Laird.

A pigeon was cooing, coo-coo, coo-coo-coo, the cushie-doo went cooing. That was something a man could understand.

"You're right, George," said the Laird, although Geordie had not stated an opinion. "Life has always meant trouble in those times and these." The Laird tut-tutted to himself. "And you and your dear wife Jean have endured your share."

He was thinking of the death of their first son, George, in the same year that Charlie was born. The death and the birth that followed it. Now they came to the place where two paths met above Geordie's cottage, to the very place where the Laird had brought bad news to Geordie. The dogs barked a welcome at the kennels, and they would be quiet if Geordie told them, but he did not tell them.

Jean would be cooking dinner in the cottage, and the shadow of grief be with her, always with her every day. She did not speak of it, and nor did he, but Geordie knew. For himself, the worst memory had faded, except occasionally, like at this moment, at this very place. . . . And again the Laird held the drowned bairn's body, and again the Laird was saying to himself, the poor Laird was praying to himself. . . . He was the one who suffered the most, Geordie thought. They had never stood together at this place since that day fifteen years ago.

But now they waited for Charlie's essay. Now Geordie watched for his other son to come. He would come round from the back door of the cottage, and beyond that was the road, and up the road fifty yards or so from that place where Geordie and the Laird were waiting, there came someone slowly on a bicycle. She was a huge fat lassie, and her muckle legs and arms were blotchy pink, and her face was pink. Maggie Oliphant was in a way a sad sight to see amid sad thoughts.

The back door banged. "Hi, Maggie Elephant!" Charlie called.

She put one foot to the ground and she turned her head and she screamed, quivering like a jelly in some places: "You dirrty wee slimy Charlie Jock." Maggie Oliphant rode on.

The Laird drew in breath beside him, and Geordie growled. It was a long slow growl about Charles Ian MacTaggart, his other son.

"Shut up, George!"

The Laird sounded vexed, and Geordie shut up. But he stared at Charlie.

"Thank you, Charles," said the Laird. "I look forward to reading it. Well, home," he mumbled, and strode away up the path.

Geordie stared down at Charlie, and Charlie stared

up. "What is it wrong I've done the noo?" His voice cracked from the man's voice to the boy's.

But Geordie managed to say nothing. He turned his back on the heartless boy, and boys would be boys, and be fair to him—how could he know the old pain that the Laird and his father had been sharing? "Quiet!" Geordie called to the dogs, still barking a welcome from the kennels; and the dogs were quiet.

★ 2 ★

It seemed that the Laird was right about Charlie just going through a difficult phase in growing up. All the next year he stuck to his lessons, and passed his "O" levels with good marks and was selected to go on for his Higher Certificate. In the summer holidays the Laird employed him at forestry work, and he did a grand job. True, he would not enter long-distance races to encourage Geordie's secret ambition for him. And he would not take up the pipes again, another ambition, a small one, of Geordie's—to have a real piper in the family. But you couldn't expect everything all at once. Charlie worked hard with his mind and body, was decent mostly to his mother, and got into no mischief worth speaking of. *He's doing fine,* Geordie said to Jean. *Yes,* she said. *If it's not just too good to last.*

But it turned out that Jean was right, and Geordie wrong. I'm the one who is always wrong, Geordie thought when the change came over Charlie again. Something happened his first day back at school. You could hear it that evening in the slam of the door, and Jean looked quickly up from her knitting, and there again was the look on Charlie's face. It was his black look of discontent that both of them feared and did not mention, hoping that it would be gone to-morrow. But it had come to stay, and once again there were awkward silence-laden meals in Geordie's house. The young never know the power they wield. The unknown demon lurked in Charlie, inside himself, against himself, against the world? How could you tell?

But nothing happened. Charlie came home and ate his supper and went up to his room and came down to the bathroom and up again to bed without saying good night if he could avoid that, and he caught the early bus to school. He had been a quick, happy boy with friends. Now he wanted no friends. In the evenings through September and October until the end of summer time, Charlie never went out.

Was he doing his studies? One evening Geordie gathered courage, climbed the stairs, knocked on the door for politeness and went in, and there was Charlie on his bed, his boots still on, reading a paperbacked book with a picture of a female in some underclothes, supposed to be great literature by a famous author, and Geordie said: "You should be at your lessons."

Charlie did not answer. He bared his teeth in a silent snarl and went back to reading, and his father retreated. He had seen that snarl in vicious dogs, and on television, and once or twice in real-life people too. "I'm feared," Jean said. "It's him not speaking that makes me feared. When I said to him: *What's the matter, Charlie? Is something not right at the school?* he just turned his back. So I got vexed, I'm sorry. It's just hopeless for you and me to speak. Would the Laird have a word with Charlie? He's aye had a grand opinion of the Laird. Could we ask the Laird to do it?"

"No," Geordie said. "The Laird's that mad at the

Hydro people, it's all he can think of, the bee in his bonnet. The Laird's in no condition even to listen to me ask him. Besides, it's our business, not the Laird's."

"Well, the Minister, then? He's a good old soul, and that's his job."

The Rev. Mr. MacNab was certainly willing to have a word with Charlie. But Charlie said: "What for would I go and see him, old giggle-giggle preaching what I don't believe, and nor does he."

"You take that back." Geordie's right hand twitched.

"I'll take it back about him, not me."

"Your beliefs are your own," Geordie said. "And you're a spoilt wee brat. No man mocks another man's beliefs."

"Is tha' a faact?" Charlie said. He spoke broad, which was an impertinence too, it not being his usual speech nowadays.

"I should have taken the stick to him," Geordie said. "That's what I should have done."

"To other boys, mebbe, not to Charlie. The two times in his life you skelped him, he just got worse. Remember?"

Geordie remembered well. What was this dark demon in their son? Did it come from Jean? Did it come from him? Where did it come from?

Jean laid her head against Geordie's jacket. Now there were grey hairs in the black, and Jean was true and as bonny to him as ever. "It's awful to say it," she said, "but I just wish he'd do something bad and explode it mebbe right out of himself. Anything would be better than these scowls and grudges. What about?"

It was at that moment on a Friday night at seven o'clock that quiet steps came downstairs from Charlie's room, and no sound on the stone floor of the scullery, and then the back door clicked softly. "Will I stop him?"

"No. Just see if he takes his bike."

Geordie heard the clank of a mudguard at the shed, and then down at the road the lights came on. A red light moved off Drumfechan way.

Jean knitted a jersey, a blue one for the boy. "It matches his eyes." She was all woman, was Jean, and she smiled a moment and stopped knitting and frowned and the needles clicked on.

Geordie was reading James Bond in the West Indies. It was Charlie's, and Geordie didn't just like the idea of a boy of sixteen reading the torture, etcetera, but what could you do? Geordie was a James Bond fan himself, and when Charlie was in his right mind they had some laughs about Bond's adventures. But to-night thoughts kept interrupting him, thoughts about violence that really did happen. It could happen at Drumfechan too. He put down the book.

"What's the time?" Jean said.

"It's after eight."

"Trouble," she said. "I know. I can feel it."

Jean had those fey feelings, and sometimes they were right, and a small shiver was in Geordie's back at hearing her say that; and he went into the room to see what was on television, but it was fights—not Wild West fights, which were a kind of old-fashioned blood-spilling joke. These were gang fights in the city, good guys pulping bad guys with the buckles of their belts. The *good guys* now, it was a twisted world of hate out there. There was a thrill to it too, a dirty pleasure in watching the good guy's buckle thud, whistle, thud, that'll teach the bad guy, lying unconscious. Too much. Geordie turned the TV off.

"Hating," he said. "I don't remember hating much when I was young. Do you?"

"I used to get mad at Geordie MacTaggart whiles. But mebbe that wasn't just hating quite." Jean laughed, putting down her knitting, and she came over to him and stood on tiptoe, her arms round his neck, and he lifted her right up by the waist to hold her to him, to kiss together. It was a long strong kiss that told the strength of them together. "We'll have to wait up for him," she said.

Geordie needed a job to pass the time, so he whittled wood to make pegs for snares. The rabbits were coming back in the glen. Time dragged on past nine, past half past nine, a quarter to ten. It had begun to rain out there, and rain sizzled in the kitchen chimney.

Jean went to turn down their bed and Charlie's. When she came back she couldn't settle, fiddled at the stove, fiddled out at the sink. "It must be our blame," she said from the scullery. "It must be our fault some way he's like he is."

You getting vexed at him is part of it, Geordie thought, but he did not say anything.

"I know what you're thinking," she called through. "You're thinking it's me and my bad temper. Well, mebbe being vexed isn't as bad as being too patient and perfect all the time, and expecting a hot-headed laddie to be that too."

"Mebbe you're right," Geordie said, avoiding the

argument that being worried made Jean want. Just
then the dogs started barking, and he went out to
stand in the open front porch. There was a full moon
behind cloud, so the night was not dark. The rain
went on and the dogs still barked and he did not call
to stop them. At this time of night they barked for
some good reason—at the scent of a fox, at people
about? Now they stopped, and now Geordie heard
what they had been barking at—it was the sound of
someone running. The dogs had recognised the
runner by the sound, as Geordie did soon.

The even thud of rubber-soled boots slowed down.
Geordie's eyes had grown accustomed to darkness, and
he saw Charlie stop just above the cottage. He
breathed in short gasps, bending over. Charlie could
run a mile, two miles at speed, and never pant like that.
He went round and in the back door. Then there were
voices, but the bath started running and Geordie could
not make out what they said. He waited outside a
little longer. Let Jean talk to him. Charlie would
sometimes tell things to her.

He went in when the taps stopped running. Jean
had Charlie's green sweater and plus fours on chairs
before the kitchen range, and they were steaming.
There was an untidy tear in one sleeve of the jersey.
"I'll need to darn it," she said.

"Well?" he said, seeing the pinched look in her face.

"He's just exhausted, and his eyes are wild. He's
been up to mischief, I ken that fine, but he says somebody let the air out of both his tyres, and he had no
pump and Storrar's Garage was closed, so he hid the
bike in the laurel bushes near the Manse and he ran
home by the Green Avenue."

"Who was he with all that time?"

"He said he wasn't with anybody."

"Away for more than three hours on a cold night and not with anybody?"

"That's what he says."

The bathroom door opened, and Charlie went upstairs. "I don't like it," Geordie said. "I'll have to speak . . ."

"Leave him be," she said. "Speak in the morning."

They went to bed, and the lights were out in Geordie's house. "It's raining again," she said. "I knew it was too early for snow to last."

"It didn't snow," Geordie said.

"There was snow on the shoulders of his jersey."

The Green Avenue, the way Charlie said that he had taken home, ran along the side of the glen, no higher up than Geordie's cottage. Snow there and not here?

Jean slept first, and then Geordie felt sleep stealing over him, and they slept together. It was big good guy Bond coming for small bad guy Geordie with belt and buckle, and Bond was shaking a bell in his other hand. "I'll go," Jean said.

Geordie's watch said ten to twelve, a fine time for folk to be telephoning. Their line came through the Big House exchange. He listened to Jean in the kitchen. She did not say much. "Hallo," she said, and then: "*What?*" And there was a long listening pause. "At five past nine. Aye, I'm sure."

"I knew it," Jean said, back in bed again, sitting up, her knees drawn to meet her chin. "The Laird put Constable Grigg through to us. The Hydro

Manager's car was . . . was taken from outside the Drumfechan Arms."

"When?"

"He went into the hotel at eight; and it was gone at half past." Jean's voice was muffled against her knees. "So they put out the alarm. And next the Bobby up at Drumfechanhead saw a car going fifty or sixty through the thirty mile limit, and it turned left into Altnadean, and they called a wireless car in from the other way to head it off, and they chased a car back over the hill road to the old quarry, where it was abandoned at nine thirty-five. But they came on and made one arrest on the hill, but they think there were two."

"Who was arrested?"

"He wouldn't say," Jean said. She was crying.

"And what did you say about five past nine?"

"I said Charlie was home at five past nine."

"Charlie came home at five past ten."

Jean shook her head. "I know," she said.

"So you told a lie."

"He's my bairn. Why wouldn't I lie to protect my own bairn?"

Geordie said nothing. He wouldn't lie to protect his own bairn, or would he? Jean lay down and turned away, and Geordie doused the lamp in their room. She stopped crying soon, but she lay too still to be asleep. It was five miles and a bit from the quarry down to here, and the police had reached the stolen car at nine thirty-five. Yes, he might just do it with a full moon behind clouds. Geordie was a long time going to sleep again.

✻ 3 ✻

"He won't even stir. Will I let him sleep?"

"Let him sleep till nine; then get him up. After breakfast send him for his bike. Don't ask any questions till I get back. Understand?"

"Yes, Geordie," she said. "Where are you going? You're not going to the pollisman?"

"I'll be back," he said.

Geordie did not take the hill road. He climbed a shorter way, straight out of the glen, through twisted birches and dead wet bracken, over the wall that marked the division of valley and hill. It was a bright morning and soon, at the thousand-foot level or so, he came to a melting skim of snow on the heather. Geordie pushed on fast. He was not the build for a long-distance runner; he was the build of a man to walk all day with a load on his back, not noticing it. He passed the first crest to circle the big bog, to climb the steep face to the Lum, which was a column or chimney of rock, with a cave at its base where you could find shelter. Now a last dip, a last climb to join the hill road winding up to the pass between Drum-fechan and Altnadean.

Here, at two thousand feet, there were three inches of new snow, pure and unbroken by any tracks. Down in the valley the rain had begun at a quarter to ten last night, so the snow might have started on the hill then too.

Geordie reached the old quarry from which had come the metal for this road. The quarry had been closed these many years, wired off because of the danger that people and beasts might blunder in to drown in the deep holes of the quarry. Now the snow had melted from the wire. Geordie looked carefully and found nothing. It was no good searching the ground in three inches of snow.

He followed the hill road for home, the white Highlands massed before him. A party of birds flew past twittering. They were snow buntings, birds of the storms and barren places.

The snow soon petered out downhill. The road was damp but the surface hard, no tracks of tyres or boots. There was one other possible place, and he came to it, the gate across the road to keep sheep and Highland cattle on the hill. It was shut always, a heavy old gate badly hung. So if you were on foot, and you knew that gate, you did not bother to open it, much quicker to hold the hinge-post, put one foot in a crack on the wall beside, the other on the single barbed wire strand on top, and vault it, simple.

Geordie searched again, and this time he found what he was looking for. He was not too bad a detective after all. But he was none too happy as he came into the valley of Drumfechan and left the hill road at Oliphant the shepherd's cottage.

"Hallo, Mr. MacTaggart."

Geordie was so deep in the trouble of his thoughts that he had not noticed the girl beside the shed. Her bicycle was upside down, and she was cleaning the spokes. With blue jeans and jersey too short and tight for her, and all the bulges and the chins, Maggie Oliphant was a sight to make you feel uneasy just looking at her. She was a decent lassie too. "Hallo, Maggie," he said. "Cleaning the bike, I see."

"Aye," she said. "It was a dirty night, coming home from the social."

The social at the Parish Hall, and the night was dirty. Would the question be dirty? Ask it. "Our Charlie was in. Did you happen to see him?"

"Not at the social, Mr. MacTaggart." Maggie Oliphant bent over the wheel. And she said, looking at the wheel: "I saw him and Tam Burrell crossing the Square."

"In the rain, that would be," Geordie said, as for conversation.

"Och no, it was early." Maggie glanced over her shoulder at him. *Maggie Elephant*, on the panty bloomers. She glanced at Charlie's father as innocently, as blankly, as wickedly as any woman can. "The clock had just chimed for half past seven," she said.

"Cheerio then, Maggie." Getting her to tell tales for a grudge against his own boy—was that fair? He walked on.

"Oh, Mr. MacTaggart!"

"Yes, Maggie?"

"Mr. MacTaggart, there's a teachers' conference one day this next week, I'm not sure which but mebbe Friday, and I was wondering if I have the day off school and you were going after the hinds could I mebbe come like you said sometime I could?" She was blushing, the poor shy muckle lassie.

"Tell us the day when you know it," Geordie said, "and we'll see what the plans are."

"Och, thanks!" she said. "Thanks, Mr. Mac-Taggart."

He met the Laird on the way home. They exchanged greetings and silence fell. The Laird puffed out his thin cheeks, a sign that he was bothered in mind. Geordie waited for the Laird's impatient nature to make him speak first.

"An unearthly hour for that damned policeman to telephone. But he told me the gist of it before I put him through to you. Awkward, George, or not?"

"Yessir." Geordie told what Charlie had said to his mother, and the state he was in when he came home, and that Geordie had not yet questioned him.

"That policeman has. He was knocking at your door when I went down earlier, so I retreated."

"Does the Laird know who the one was they arrested?"

"Tam Burrell," said the Laird. "He says he was alone, I gather."

Tam Burrell was the barman's son at the public bar of the Drumfechan Arms, and he and Charlie had been in trouble before, not serious trouble like this.

The Laird coughed, more information coming. "There are other complications," he said. "Six empty bottles of strong ale to meet the Minister this morning."

"At the door of the Manse?"

"No, in a row across the chancel steps. Not too good a one, eh, George?"

Geordie did not and could not answer.

"Things are not entirely black, though. MacNab is truly a turner of the Christian cheek. And that Hydro feller, I had a word with him, pointed out that the car was facing homewards, after all."

"It was chased homewards," Geordie said.

"Well, perhaps. But no damage to it, and young Burrell has a driving licence, and no question of real . . . er theft. And his own conscience is so damned guilty about the monstrous conduct of his men. Know what they did last night?"

Geordie shook his head.

"They went and beat up the forestry crew. God knows I have little use for the Forestry Commission, but their men are good types. Dirty caitiffs, and this poaching . . ."

"I'll sort them if I catch them poaching," Geordie said.

"So the long and the short of it is that the car owner will not press charges. Innocent or less so, I think young Charles will get away with it."

"Not with me, he won't," Geordie said.

"You won't be too hard on him, George? They explode at that age, y'know, they go bang. Don't you remember?"

"I don't remember stealing cars, nor drinking beer in the Kirk."

"No proof he did, y'know. No proof he did."

"I'll soon find out."

Puff-puff went the Laird's thin cheeks. "I had a word with Jean just now. She seems very upset."

"Jean told the pollisman that Charlie came in at five past nine when he wasn't home till after ten o'clock."

"Couldn't it have been nine?"

"No, sir, it could not."

"The best women don't fight for their kith and kin by Queensberry rules. The best women aren't gentlemen, George, let's face it."

"I don't see a joke in Jean telling lies to save Charlie's skin." Geordie's slow anger was growing in him—with the Laird, with Jean, with Charlie, with himself. "I will work this afternoon to make up the Laird's work-time I've wasted," he said, and he left the Laird.

The Laird of Drumfechan watched his gamekeeper stride off. "What a monument of truth and honour, to truth and honour," the old Laird muttered. "And rustic Jehovah's blood is up. Poor Charles and Jean."

"I sent him for his bike, like you said."

"The Laird says the pollisman was here. What did Charlie tell him?"

"They were in the room, and the door was shut, so I didn't hear just right."

"What did you hear?"

"He said he went to the post office for a chocolate bar, and left his bike outside, and then he went for a walk alone down the river when the moon first came up and the sky was still clear, and he saw an otter."

"Was he with Tam Burrell?"

"He said he never saw Tam Burrell."

"Maggie Oliphant saw him cross the Square with Tam Burrell at half past seven, the clock had just chimed." Geordie looked at Jean. "They drank beer in the Kirk and left six empty bottles."

"Och, no!" she said. "Och, no! I smelt the beer

on him too, and I didn't want to say, so as not to make
more trouble."

"What else didn't you want to say so as not to make
more trouble?"

"That's all," she said. "Och, Geordie, please."

"And your fairy story about nine o'clock—did you
stick to that?"

Jean nodded.

"And Charlie took the lie up from you, and said
nine o'clock?"

Jean nodded. She was afraid of him. In their
twenty-three years she had never shown fear of him,
and he had not wanted to have her afraid, but now . . .

The back door opened, and Charlie went up. "Get
him here," Geordie said. "And you come too."

They came back in a minute. Geordie sat in a
chair, and so did Jean. She looked guiltier than Charlie.
He was pale and calm; he did not look guilty, not
even hostile. Charlie was a handsome boy, a few spots
round his chin. He was close-knit and supple, not a
loose-limbed laddie who would grow tall.

"Tell me what happened last night from the time
you left here till the time you got back."

Geordie let him tell it without questions—the
chocolate bar at the P.O. and sweetie shop, and the
moon came up and the stars were out, he went down
the river bank, down the line of big beeches to look
for an otter, and he saw one, swimming and diving,
hunting a salmon in the moonlit river—Charlie told
it well enough to make you see that otter. Some time
or other he must have seen that otter. And then the
sky clouded over and he went back to the village, but
his bike was gone, and it took him a long time to find

it in Lady's Wynd, and the tyres were flat and everything closed, so he hid it in those laurel bushes, and then he came home through sleet and rain by the Green Avenue.

"What time were you home?"

"At the back of nine, Mum said. My watch is bust."

"And that was all you did last night?"

Charlie looked him straight in the eye. "Yes, Dad," he said.

"You never went drinking beer with Tam Burrell in the Kirk?"

"No, Dad."

"You never saw Tam Burrell?"

"No, Dad."

"You never took the car and went along the road by the loch to Drumfechanhead and up to Altnadean?"

"No, Dad."

"You never took the hill road with the police car after you, and left it at the old quarry?"

"No, Dad."

"You never ran away and left your slow pal to be caught?"

His eyes flickered to that, to that at last. "No, Dad."

"Jean," he said, "have you had to mend his green jersey afore?"

She looked at him, afraid of him. She shook her head. "Just this morning," she said.

Geordie took the wallet from his inside pocket and opened it. "How come, then," he said, "that I found this wool on the barbed wire by the hill gate?"

Charlie sighed. It was a long shuddering sigh of

relief to be freed of the lies that hemmed him in. He said nothing, looking down. He swayed and said nothing.

Geordie pushed out a kitchen chair. "Here, sit down," he said in quite a kindly way. He hadn't finished with him. He hadn't got started with him. He looked at the traces of ink still on Charlie's hands.

"So he took your fingerprints?"

Charlie nodded.

"That's a fine credit to the family. Did you leave prints on the bottles?"

Charlie shook his head. "We wiped them off."

Of course they would have wiped them off. These days they learned all about crime at six. "So you wiped the bottles off and left them to desecrate the Kirk."

"We didn't mean it about the Kirk. There was nowhere else to go, Dad."

"Nowhere else to go. I wonder you didn't throw the bottles through the stained-glass window."

"Please, Geordie."

But he paid no heed. "And the beer. Did you steal that too?"

"Tam . . . We got them at the shed behind. It wasn't like stealing, not from his dad."

"Do you steal from me?"

Charlie broke down to the strangled desperate sobs of sixteen, and Geordie was sorry, but he hadn't finished with him yet. "Stop greeting and go wash your face and come back here."

They sat in silence for five minutes, for ten, until Charlie came back. He had stopped crying, only just. He gave a shudder, after crying.

"Now get on your bike and ride in and tell Constable Grigg the truth like a man, all the truth. Then come back here, if he lets you come."

"What about the time I got home, if he asks me?"

"Say your mother made a mistake, it was after ten. She did," Geordie added.

"I did not," Jean said.

"One thing you needn't say is about the wool from your jersey. He wouldn't like it was me who found the evidence, not him. Now hurry up."

"Will they bring charges against him, Geordie?"

"No," he said. "The Laird's seen to that, without asking me."

"The Laird is decent," she said. "The Laird understands what takes a laddie." She looked at him, afraid of him. "What are you going to do?"

"I'm going to give him a hiding," Geordie said. "That's what I'm going to do."

"But he's sorry, Geordie. You can see he's just bursting with being sorry. It's all washed out of him. A hiding would just start . . ."

"I'm his father," Geordie said. "They can let him off, and you can tell lies for him. That's their business and yours, not mine. I know my business."

"Aye," she said. "You always know that."

Geordie went out to cut an ash stick, strong enough not to break, thin enough to hurt, not thick enough to damage.

"We'll wait for our dinner till Charlie gets back," he said.

It was nearly one when Charlie came in. His head was up, and his eye met Geordie's, and the devil was washed out of him, and he was ashamed. "I'm sorry, Dad," he said in the kitchen.

Geordie grunted. "Come on," he said. "Let's get it over with."

Charlie was startled. He hadn't expected to get what he had earned. But he followed Geordie into the room and he bent over the chair as he was bidden, and he took six strokes without sound or movement. They were at about half Geordie's strength, but hard enough.

"Is that all?"

"Yes," Geordie said. "That's finished and done with as far as I'm concerned."

They went back to the kitchen where poor Jean was standing. Charlie looked at her and said: "I'm sorry, Mum. You're decent." Then he turned to his father and said quietly: "You could have said that about the wool from my jersey. But you didn't. You made me tell all those lies again just to prove I'm a disgrace and you're so perfect. I take it all back about being sorry. I hate you."

* 4 *

If Jean was afraid of Geordie that Saturday morning, she was not afraid of him that Saturday afternoon when he came back from making up lost work.

"Charlie's away to Uncle Jim's. He's to spend the week there."

"Who says he's to spend the week at Uncle Jim's?"

"I just wonder who." Jean was quick to be vexed and quick to smile. But that was the surface Jean. This was another one. "Would you be having any objections?"

Geordie cleaned his gun. He had waited a long time for those hoodies, a right and left at hooded crows, not bad. And all the wait he had been thinking how he would make it up with Charlie. *Let bygones be bygones. You did wrong and you paid for it, and there's one thing I want you to promise me, and that's never to tell a lie again, never in your life except mebbe a white lie for the sake of kindness.* And: *Sorry, Charlie, if I did wrong too.* But now he was cheated of that. He stood his shotgun in the rack. "Why did you send him to Uncle Jim's?"

"To get him away from you," she said. "Surely even the great Geordie would know that."

"Aye," Geordie said, "away from the father he hates."

"He didn't mean to say it. He meant he hated the way you led him on to cheat him."

"I had to find the truth," Geordie said. "So I had to hear his story."

"Did you have to ask him all yon questions, make him lie and lie and lie again, and you with the evidence to break him, the wool in your pocket? Wasn't that cheating him?"

"I told you—I was trying to get at the truth when he'd done wrong. Is that cheating?"

"And yon Maggie Oliphant—getting her to tell on him for spite. Wasn't that cheating?"

"Mebbe so," he said. "But did you not cheat Charlie worse when you told a lie to save him from punishment he deserved?"

"There you go again," Jean said, her back to Geordie at the window, his bonny wife who hated him too. And what was this hating? Hadn't they loved together for the two boys they loved, the one they had lost, and the one they were losing? And if right was wrong, and wrong was right . . .

"How do you mean: *There you go again?*" Life was a sore perplexing muddle.

Jean turned. "Do you know what Charlie said to me; he said: *I've got a new name for Dad: it's P squared, P to the power of two. Perfection personified, that's Dad.*"

"And you said: *That's a rich one, Charlie. That's a real good joke.*"

"I said: *He doesn't mean to be. He doesn't think it about himself. Dad's not stuck up, or the like of that. Dad just can't help it.* And Charlie said: *Dad's a grand good man, and I know it every day. But Dad's so perfect he isn't human. What use is a perfect dad to me?*"

All the next week Geordie drove himself extra hard to escape the sins of his perfection. And as for being perfect, like Jean and Charlie seemed to think, he was the worst sinner that he knew; so then he must be a hypocrite, which was worse. He was not used to thinking about himself, the judge questioning the perfect criminal inside, and good was bad, and all mixed up.

It was the back of the year, that time when the stalking of stags was over, but the deer were too plentiful, so the worthless had to be shot and hinds reduced in number. On Monday and Tuesday Geordie rode his motor bike to get quickly on to the hill. It was a special cross-country bike that the Laird had bought from Germany, strong enough to carry twenty stone pretty well anywhere. He left the bike on the hill road, and spied for parcels of hinds—they were not high at this time of year—and then he went stalking them on foot.

Wednesday and Thursday he had worked in the glen, getting ready for the Laird's first pheasant shoot a week come Saturday. On Friday Charlie was to come home after school, and that lay like a shadow beyond the day ahead.

Jean had not been too bad to Geordie all week, just a bit standoffish, or old-fashioned as the Laird would say. "You're good to take yon poor lassie," she said.

"Och, she's company," Geordie said. The company of Maggie Oliphant would be mostly puffing and panting as she lumbered after him. But he had to watch his tongue, not admitting that it might be good of him.

"Hop on," he said at the shepherd's cottage. With

Maggie riding the pillion, Geordie needed one gear lower than usual on the hill road. But she opened and closed the gate for him, which was a help, and soon they were over the first crest. He drew out the telescope. "The wind's steady from the east," he said. "That's the way we should try." Geordie spied the glen. There were beasts all over, too many beasts for a stalk to be possible at any single lot, unless . . . "Here, you take a look," he said. "See the bare face with the white patch of quartz? Just below that."

"Two old hinds," Maggie said. "And four with calves, and one wee staggie. But how would we get at them, Mr. MacTaggart?"

"If they stay lying down, we can," he said. "First, we go up the bed of the burn to the rocks where you see the water splashing, syne there's a long peat hag to the left. Easy to there, but the last bit's a flat crawl, or those ones will be on to us." He pointed across to the south face of the glen, and thought about a flat crawl with Maggie.

In a man's cloth cap, and a short duffel coat for her upper parts, and the bluejeans and the wellington boots, she was outsized in all directions. "Mr. Mac-Taggart, how can you be sure of all that you can't even see?" Maggie was not doubting his knowledge. It was admiration pure and simple.

"Och well," he said. "I was raised on the hill."

They followed the burn and then were in the dank dark peat hag, and Maggie was his faithful shadow, not puffing much. The wind was cold from the east.

"It's a crawl now," Geordie whispered. "A hundred yards of a belly crawl. Mebbe you'd better bide here."

"Och, couldn't I come? I can crawl fine on my belly, Mr. MacTaggart."

"Okay, then. Keep down." He meant *keep that muckle bottom down*, but he didn't quite like to say a rude-sounding thing to hurt her feelings.

So Geordie made the slow tiring stalk, and Maggie stayed right up behind him. She gasped so much that he looked round to see if it was proving too much for her. She was crimson in the face, but she could crawl fine on her belly, no doubt of that. "I'm okay," she panted. "Go on!" Maggie was game, keen as mustard.

He drew off the rifle cover, rested a minute, signed to her to stay where she was, and went on to do his job. He fired three shots. Geordie stood. All over the hill deer galloped into wind. He and Maggie walked up to the three dead beasts, two old hinds, and a young stag, a switch that would never make anything of a head.

He took off his jacket and rolled up his sleeves. Maggie Oliphant did likewise. "I'll help," she announced. With Geordie wielding the knife, and Maggie coming after him, the gralloch was quickly done. "Look!" she said, holding up the first shattered heart. "Look!" she said, holding up the second. "Look!" she said, holding up the third in her bloody hand, blood to the elbows. "Man, Mr. MacTaggart, that's just grand shooting at two hundred yards."

"Not too bad," he said. The not too bad could hardly be better.

They dragged the beasts below the white patch of quartz where the pony man would find them. Then they went down to the burn to wash off blood.

"Not too tired?" Geordie said.

"Och no, Mr. MacTaggart. But I was fair sweatin'. I took off mebbe five or six pounds I could afford to be taking." Maggie laughed. It was nice her being able to laugh at herself, a lassie so huge that the world made a joke of her. But to be able to laugh is not to like being laughed at, Geordie thought, remembering the hate in her voice last year: *You dirrty wee slimy Charlie Jock*. Charlie was coming back to-night, and that *hating* word. I did right, Geordie thought. "What else could I do?" he said aloud by mistake.

Maggie looked quickly at him and did not speak. She's my pal, Geordie thought, my elephant pal, with some unkindness in his thoughts about the world and everyone, including Maggie. "It's cold," he said. "We could eat our sandwiches at the Lum."

The wind had a bite, and the sky was grey, and occasional flakes of snow came from the east, but no snow was lying. He and Maggie ate their sandwiches in the small damp cave that was called the Lum for the chimney above it. The Lum became quite cosy when they shared Geordie's Thermos of strong tea.

"I hear it's a teacher you're to be," he said.

"That's what I'd like," she said. "And Mum has a new idea—that I might go to my Auntie Ella's in New Zealand and learn to be a teacher there."

"New Zealand—that's a grand country, by the reputation."

"A grand country for the fat girl," Maggie said. There was bitterness in her. "What would your opinion be of teaching, Mr. MacTaggart?"

"A fine profession," Geordie said, "for folk with the intelligence. And you have that."

"What's intelligence?" Maggie said glumly. "But

that's all I have, so a teacher I'll be, mebbe in New Zealand."

"Well, you've got your mind made up, which is a good thing. Our Charlie can't decide what he's to do."

The faintest hiss from Miss Oliphant told her opinion of Charlie MacTaggart. So Geordie led his mind and hers away from the subject. "That's a bad gang at the Hydro Scheme," he said.

"Just awful, Mr. MacTaggart. Two of the forestry men are to be in hospital another week, so I hear tell. That was Cooligan did that."

"Cooligan?"

"He's the one that makes the trouble. He's a real big dirty beast, is Cooligan. Not as big as you, of course, Mr. MacTaggart."

"Not as big a dirty beast as me?"

Maggie's laugh boomed heartily in the Lum. "Gosh, Mr. MacTaggart, you're a scream."

"This Cooligan—how come you know him?"

"I don't know him, Mr. MacTaggart. I've just seen him the once, I was on my bike, him swaggering with a bunch of cronies, and he said . . ."

"What, Maggie?"

Maggie Oliphant blushed. Geordie could feel the heat of her blushing in the Lum, but that might be his imagination. "I'm no' saying," she said. Then Maggie spat. She vented her feelings with a bull's-eye jet of spittle right out through the rocky door of the Lum. "He's one I hate," she said.

"That's a grand spit you have."

"Aye," she said. "I was champion in my spitting days."

She could crawl on her belly and gralloch a stag and spit like a champion, and she hated Cooligan, whoever he might be. There was still more to this lassie than met the eye.

"Why was the constable not there to stop the fight?"

"Yon Constable Grigg!" Maggie said.

"H'mm," Geordie agreed.

"Besides," she said, frowning, "that was Friday when the car was stolen."

Maggie Oliphant used the right word, *stolen*, and his son stole it. Och, come on now, Geordie said to himself. "Come away then," he said to her, and they went out.

In half an hour the wind had veered almost into the south and it was warmer. "That's good," Geordie said. "We can try the west side now."

They crossed the hill road. Soon it began to drizzle. "It's the Highland weather," Geordie said. There were many kinds of Highland weather—the fierce and the balmy, the rain and the snow. But drizzle might be the most Highland weather.

"It's the quietness I like," Maggie said. "And the tops all hidden. Are the tops still there, you might ask yourself."

Geordie knew the feeling. His faithful shadow followed him. When he stopped, so did she. When he spoke, so did she. She was no bother. There were beasts here and there, but they were skeery in the changing weather. No sooner did you see the chance of a stalk than they would move restlessly again. The clouds came lower.

"We'd better . . ." Geordie was going to say that

they had better make for home, but he did not say it.
The shot echoed up and round and back, and the
echoes died. But the first sound had come from the
shoulder of the West Tully, just below the clouds.
Now there was a second shot. They were muffled,
and yet they could not be far away in that direction.

"Poachers," he said. "That'll be the night shift
poaching. Maggie, you walk back to the road. Walk
fast to get there before the mist comes down. Stay at
the bike. Don't move from the road, or you'll be
lost."

"I couldn't be lost if I stayed with you."

"They're a tough bunch, those. There could be
trouble."

"What's trouble?" Maggie said. "Please, Mr. Mac-
Taggart." Her brown eyes pleaded.

"Keep up then." Geordie went at a walk and run
to cut them off. He had not heard a shot the other
time, but ravens had led him to a day-old gralloch;
and then he had followed the drag downhill off the
moor through woods to the lochside where they had
skinned the beast and cut it up. He found the skin
buried. Geordie had told no one, not even the Laird.
He respected good poachers, but not the kind who
would take a red-deer calf for an easy drag. Now here
was the chance he had been waiting for. It was the
perfect chance to catch them red-handed if the mist
did not beat him to it.

A sheep path followed the contour of the hill and
made good going. Maggie kept up pretty well.
A stout lassie, for all her stoutness, Geordie thought.
Then he was over the shoulder and down beyond,

down to the edge of the shallow gully which they
would have to follow with the beast, if they had a beast.
Geordie stopped beside it. Did he hear sounds farther
up? Then Maggie arrived.

"Bide you here," he said. "Lie clappit behind the
rock. Not a move, not a sound until I call."

"But, Mr. MacTaggart!"

"Do as I tell ye."

He went up the gully and found a good hiding-
place, and took the rifle from its cover. He heard them
coming. They had to come this way because the hill
on both sides was a tangle, a currycomb of broken
rock.

Geordie did not get up until the men were almost
on him. "Stand where you are," he said. They were
a tough-looking pair, a short broad bandy-legged
one; the other taller with pale eyes, he held a rifle
slung—it was a carbine with a silencer. Geordie held
his own at the point of balance in his right hand.
"Lay the rifle down," he said. "Lay it down with the
butt to me."

"Who would you be to be giving orders?" The
thin man's hand tightened on the sling. He was a
dangerous man, Geordie knew, a kind of man beyond
Geordie's experience, but he knew. And he knew he
could be quicker than that man.

"Lay it down, I said."

The man did as he was told.

"Now stand away, the pair of you."

They obeyed him. Then Geordie saw that the red-
deer calf was moving feebly. There was a froth, a
bloody bubbling from its lips, and the eye had suffering
life in it. He shot it through the head. The short

man gave a start, and the deer lay still, and the thin man did not stir.

"So you would drag a live beast," Geordie said.

"The fog came down," the short one said. *Daown*, he said, an Englishman. "We couldn't 'elp it." He was scared. He didn't look too bad a wee chap.

"It was dyin' onyway," said the other. "So what's the difference?"

"Cruelty," Geordie said. "Have you heard of that?" His neck prickled about the cold thin man as he walked over for the rifle and went back to where he had been standing. Geordie laid his own rifle down. The other was American, a thirty-thirty or the like, with a Martini action, a useful weapon at short range. Or it had been before Geordie snapped it in two across his knee, and threw the butt and the rest of it away. "That's for dragging live beasts," he said. He felt a bit better, and the pieces clattered somewhere in the mist.

"You'll pay for that," the thin man said.

"Name?" Geordie said. The short one's name was Borton.

"Name?" he said again.

"What's yours?" The thin man was not afraid.

"My name's MacTaggart," Geordie said gently.

"Well I never, it's Geordie MacTaggart, King Kong himself."

"H'ssht," from Borton.

"Say yon again," Geordie said.

The man's hand was straying to be near a sheath knife on his belt. "Are ye dief?"

"You are," Geordie said, and he boxed his ears, left right, full strength with the palm of each hand.

The thin man collapsed to hold his deaf ears. Geordie bent and drew out the knife, and he threw that away too. *What use is a perfect dad to me?*

"What's his name?"

"McClintock," Borton said.

Here came the mist.

"Follow the gully," Geordie said. "You can't go wrong. And you might just mention to your pals what they might be expecting if I see them on the hill."

McClintock was still dazed, but still unafraid. His cold glare wavered on Geordie, and Borton led him down.

Geordie slung the dead calf over one shoulder, his rifle from the other, and he met the loom of Maggie in the mist. "I saw everything," she said, "except your hands moved too quick to see when you boxed his ears, the dirrty cruel beast, it was like two pistol shots. Could I carry the rifle, Mr. MacTaggart?"

He let her do that. The mist was down thick. "Follow close," he said. Even a man who had known the ground all his life could mistake this hillock for that, the dangerous bog for the shallow one. Geordie checked with the small compass he carried in his buttonhole—due east was all right. But Geordie himself was not all right. *What for would I behave like yon? Smashing a rifle and boxing ears—two things I never did in my life. What's got into me? Hitting wee men, I should be ashamed.* But Geordie was not ashamed.

They came to the hill road, where he cleaned the young deer and left it. Then he and Maggie Oliphant walked down to the bike. Geordie rode it at a walking pace until they came out of the clouds. Down at home the lights were coming on for another night.

"Thanks, Maggie," he said at her house. "You were a grand help to me. Night-night."

But she lingered, blushing so fiercely he could see it in the gloaming. "Mr. MacTaggart!"

"Aye?" he said shortly.

"Och, Mr. MacTaggart, I think you're just perfect."

⋆ 5 ⋆

"Tag *thief* on a boy," said the Laird, "and the label tends to stick. That's why I used mild persuasion with the Hydro chap. Besides, it was no more stealing than my eye. They went for a berserk joy-ride. But beer in church, that's a different kettle of fish—I mean sacrilege, eh?"

The Laird and the Rev. Mr. MacNab were having a cup of tea together, or the Minister's cup held tea and milk and sugar, and the Laird's outsized cup contained a dram of whisky also.

"Bad," the Minister said gravely. "But it wasn't real sacrilege they were meaning. I talked to young Tam Burrell. First, they needed a shelter out of the cold, and the Kirk would provide that, but the Kirk was forbidden ground, so a risk and a defiance in it, and then after three bottles each of strong ale . . . Och," said the Minister, "I'd rather have a few empty bottles paraded in my Kirk on a Saturday forenoon than a lot of half-full hypocrites paraded on Sunday after a thick night of it." The Laird and the Minister laughed in the study beside the fire. "But it's worrisome about Charlie MacTaggart. There's a wayward streak."

"Yes, indeed," said the Laird. "George was perfectly right to beat the boy. What else could he do after those lies?"

"I don't know," said Mr. MacNab.

"Fact remains that the MacTaggarts are a house divided—or worse than that, they're a house united against the stalwart head of it." The Laird lowered his voice. "Even George's mother has it in for him. She says he expects too much of Charles. Jean expresses it differently—I had a word with her to-day, and she quoted young Charles: *What use is a perfect dad to me?*"

"Ticklish," said the Minister.

"He is, too, you know—the very soul of honour, kindly, humble, unselfish, follows every commandment, not by conscious obedience but inherent quality. George is my hero. He's everyone's hero, can't escape it, poor fella. George is the one I'm sorry for."

"Ticklish," said the Minister again. "It would be very wrong of a clergyman to wish that any good soul should be less good."

"Yes, it would. Now look at the state of this glen, I ask you. Until last year a refuge of peace in a hideous world. And now? Now the hooligans prevail. Now our men are beaten up, our women offended, our birds and deer molested. George won't come clean about the poaching, a law unto himself, that fella, but I know he's been keeping something from me. And as for the women, Jean herself complains that to cross Drumfechan Square is to run the gauntlet of whistle and ogle and lewd aside. A damned fine woman, Jean. I told her to mention it to her husband. But some of our ladies are perhaps not so genuinely dismayed by the attentions of these scallywags."

The Minister tutted.

"So there are more troubles cooking, if a few not

already cooked. I mean everyone's husband can't be a George; and there are some handsome scoundrels at the dam. They can work too, that I will admit. They earn their vast shekels. But rude, y'know, gratuitously rude. I happened to walk past to-day, minding my own business, head averted from the satanic inferno of their labours. Suddenly total silence, and out of it a brazen voice frae Glesca Toon: *See yon auld tattiebogle wi' the skirrt on? Yon's the Laird o' Sleepy Hollow.* And instantly work resumed. A skirted scarecrow, damned impertinence."

The Minister choked over his tea.

"Not funny. Your turn will come. And talking of turns—last Friday it was the forestry people. Last Saturday they broke up the pub. And where was that policeman? The first night he was raising a hue and cry for a couple of harmless boys. The second night he pedalled industriously away as soon as trouble started. This Friday night whose turn will it be, where will he scuttle with his notebook? Bah!"

"Whiles it takes a strong hand to restore the peace."

"My very sentiments. That policeman is a weak sister, write him off to Sleepy Hollow. There is only one hope, are we agreed?"

"It's a slender muckle hope," the Minister said.

"I think of the great St. Bernard, that patrician of the canine race, so wise, so deliberate, so kindly, wouldn't hurt a fly unless it happened to be a rat or similar vermin; so valiant, so humble, so rightly loved by all and sundry, in other words the perfect dog, ever ready to sacrifice himself in storm and blizzard for the common weal. Might he have a slow anger too? I fancy that with infinite patience a

righteous wrath might be provoked. Then wham!
Watch out, the mongrel pack!"

"The patience of Job and more would be required,
I'm thinking, to arouse St. Bernard's wrath."

"Stop giggling, man! Now listen . . ."

Soon there came a knock. It was Mrs. MacTaggart
senior. "Would the Laird be able to see Geordie now,
or should he wait?"

"Certainly, Mistress MacTaggart. Please ask him
to come along."

George MacTaggart dipped his head for the door,
and shut it behind him. He said a polite if taciturn
good evening.

"Hail, George! Mr. MacNab and I have just been
lamenting the woeful state of affairs in this glen.
Things have reached a pretty pass. Well, how did
you get on to-day?"

"I got two hinds and a switch in the forenoon.
Then the wind changed and the beasts were skeery,
and the clouds were closing in, and I was just about to
say home to Maggie Oliphant when there were two
shots over the Tully way."

"Poachers, eh?"

"Aye, poachers," Geordie said. "I caught two of
them red-handed with the calf they were dragging,
and it not even dead."

"Not dead? The swine! What did you do?"

"The one with the rifle was McClintock, and I
didn't take much of a shine to him, so I broke his
rifle at the stock to teach him to drag live beasts, and
then he gave me a bit more lip, so I boxed his ears for
him." Geordie paused, regarding the ceiling. "They'll
be singing a day or two," he said.

Beneath his field of vision, the Laird and Minister exchanged astonished glances. "Oh, I say, George! Did this rascally McClintock hit you first?"

"He did not."

"What did he say then?"

Geordie growled deeply and briefly. His majestic smoulder was impressive.

"Extreme provocation certainly, without a doubt. But in the dim eyes of the law physical violence is justified only in self-defence, I fear, eh, Mr. Mac-Nab?"

The Minister shook his head, then nodded his head in regretful agreement.

"So this could be awkward, George."

"Aye, it could. And if the Laird wants my notice he can have it."

"*Want your notice?*" The Laird jumped up and paced the room in great agitation. "*I* want your notice after all these years of impeccable service, after all these years of your shining example as a man of peace, *a verray parfit gentil knight . . . ?*"

"A verra *what?*" said Geordie.

"*Parfit*, Chaucerian English for *perfect*, y'know. And then comes a time of trouble when our very way of life is threatened, and who strikes a first blow for all the decencies that we hold dear? Provoked beyond endurance, our champion strikes not one blow but two for the sake of the glen—open-handed blows, George, no hope of skull fractures, eh?"

"No," Geordie said. "Just slaps."

"And then you have the effrontery to suggest that I might want your notice. Don't you know that I am with you through shot and shell? I mean the Minister and I may be a bit long in the tooth for the battle line, and he isn't allowed to anyway, poor chap. But our hearts are in the right place, eh, Minister, by God?"

The Minister coughed. "Well, yes," he said. "With reservations about the taking of the Lord's good name, and if I follow the drift of the Laird's eloquence aright."

"Old gasbag, you mean. Well anyway, we stand four square against the host of the Philistines. Let's have a noggin on it. Whisky, George?"

"I don't mind," Geordie said. "Schlanch!" he said, and downed the Laird's generous dram in one gulp. Geordie smacked his lips but did not unbend.

"Your throstle was too dry," said the Laird. "I wanted to propose a fervent toast: *Perdition to the Philistines.* Better have a top-up, George." They drank that toast.

"I gave Jean a lift home from the village to-day. We were comparing notes about the conduct of those ruffians. Quite scandalous, I gather, from what she would not tell me; she might be shy even to tell you."

Geordie scowled. "Maggie Oliphant was saying the same—some chap called Cooligan is the worst."

"That's the Irishman from Glasgow," said the Minister. "And a big bold buccaneer he is."

"The Oliphant girl—good gracious, even she not safe, poor child. But after all, I myself am not safe from rudeness of another nature."

"Were they rude to the Laird?"

"They certainly were. . . ."

"Tattie . . ." Geordie muttered. "Sleepy Hollow. Sleepy Hollow, eh?"

"Young Charles is due home to-night?"

"That's right," Geordie said. "On the eight o'clock bus." He coughed. "Now, if the Laird has nothing more for me . . ."

"Not a thing, George, thank you very much. I do hope you understand that I am entirely with you about striking that miserable creature. More power to you. If I seemed surprised for a moment, it was only that I didn't think you . . ."

"The Laird didn't think I had it in me?"

"Please don't blame me, George, after all these peaceful years."

"It's not the Laird I'm blaming," Geordie said, and left.

"It's either the Laird or Mephistopheles himself or both that Geordie should be blaming."

"And who was an accessory? Who was *éminence grise* while I did all the dirty work?"

"That's right," said the Minister. "And it's a heavy burden on my so-called conscience."

"Does the Christian end never justify the means?"

"Ticklish," said the Minister. That started a theological argument, most enjoyable.

Geordie strode home. It was dark, but he could follow the path by a faint difference that was sky between the trees. It was a kind of game never to slow down, never even to touch a bush beside the narrow path. It was a game you learned after a thousand times, after ten thousand times, night after night, year after year in the same sleepy hollow like a prison. But perfect gentle knights don't box dirty wee men's ears for impertinence, they turn the other

cheek, SMACK SMACK, a good bad feeling, eh? SMACK,
right into that monkey-puzzle tree. Serves you right.
Geordie took care the rest of the way.

"You're bleeding, Geordie, all down your cheek."

"It was the monkey-puzzle," he said, and went to
put his face under the scullery tap, and he came back,
cheek smarting cool outside and a glow within, and
he said: "Where's the whisky bottle?"

"In the oak chest in the room. Why, Geordie?"

"I'm wounded," he said. "I'm needing Scotch
whisky for to stop me fainting from my wounds. Awa'
and fetch it, lassie, if you please." He seated himself
in his chair by the stove.

"You haven't touched a drop since Hogmanay,
and yon was just a wee deoch an' doris."

"That's right," he said. "Would you care for a
dram?" Geordie helped himself.

"Och no," she said. "Och well, a wee one for company's sake."

"Tak off yer apron, then. Mak yersel decent for
the whisky."

Jean snorted, left the kitchen, and soon came back.
"Am I decent for the whisky?"

"You'll do," he said, pouring one for her and one
for himself. "You're a bonny wee bezzom when you
put your mind to it."

"What's got into you, Geordie?"

"Nothing that won't come out," he said. He looked
his wife over. He had her giggling and puzzled.
When did he last have her giggling and puzzled?
"You saw the Laird to-day?"

"Aye," she said. "He gave me a lift back from
Drumfechan."

"The Laird says you were complaining about the Hydro chaps."

"Och well, just mostly whistles and the like of that. Ye ken how the Laird exaggerates."

"Was there one called Cooligan?"

"Aye," Jean said. "That's the name they give him."

"And what did he say?"

"Och, nothing. I'm no' saying." Jean blushed. It was a bonny thing to see her blush.

"Come on," Geordie said. "Be a sport and tell us."

"He said, he caught me in the corner by the sweetie shop, and he said . . ."

"Och well," Geordie said. "Yon's a compliment."

"And he said: *Ask me up some time when the coast is clear. I'd like fine to poach the keeper's preserves.*"

"Did he now? And what did you say?"

"I didn't say nothin'. I socked him one, the verra idea. But he just laughed and said: *You're wastin' your time in Sleepy Hollow.*"

"So you are," Geordie said. He laughed himself, and took whisky.

"What d'you mean: *So you are. I'm wasting my time.*"

"Who isn't?" he said. "Well, mebbe I'll take a ride into the capital of Sleepy Hollow. Want to come?"

"Geordie, you're not like yourself at all."

"Want to come?"

"It's a long time since you asked me out. I'd like fine . . . Och, but Geordie, I can't. Charlie's due on the bus at eight."

"Can he not walk into the house alone?"

"And him away a week, and me not there to meet him. Och, Geordie, I couldn't."

"Suit yersel, then, perfect Mummy." He picked up his cap and coat. "Cheeri-ta-ta."

"But, Geordie . . . ! Come back, Geordie!"

Geordie MacTaggart wheeled out the bike. "I'll learn them," he said, kicking down on the starter. Learn who? He rode off through the mist to learn them.

★ 6 ★

Mist came and went on the Drumfechan road, sometimes as thick as fog, and then it would lift to be no more than a haziness beyond the headlight, and close again. It was a night to be careful, but somehow or other Geordie did not feel in the mood for caution. He knew this road well enough to ride it in the dark. Just like I knew the monkey-puzzle, he thought, his left cheek smarting in the chilly wind. He swung at a good clip into Drumfechan Square, a few lights glimmering through the mist, and who should appear but Constable Grigg with the hand of the law upraised. *That policeman*, the Laird called him. Geordie stopped in time, not without a slither of the rear wheel.

"Too fast, Mr. MacTaggart. It is a night to be observing caution."

"I was," Geordie said. "I was doing fifteen in a thirty limit."

The constable's hand drifted to his notebook pocket. "That's as may be," he said. "But the law provides that, speed limits or not, the vehicle shall at all times be driven with due regard for the public safety."

No argy-bargy wi' the policeman, was an old wise Drumfechan rule. "That's right, Officer," Geordie said. "I'll see to it in future."

There were a few lamps in the Square, one here

between the post office and the policeman's house, one at the left beside the Manse where the road to Drumfechanhead started up the south side of the loch, one at the far right corner beyond the Kirk near the Roman Brig, one back on the right at the front door of the Drumfechan Arms, one at the door to the public bar.

This left side of the Square was empty but for the constable and Geordie. Over there some men were standing by the Roman Brig, a traffic of ones and twos between that light and the bar, some strolling over to have a pint, some back to join the group of men. In the distance, up to the west of the Roman brig, were the sounds of the night shift at the Hydro Scheme—the rattle of compressors, the grumph and grind of big machines. But Drumfechan Square was quiet. "The wind's gone into the west," Geordie said. "The mist will be lifting afore long." There was the shed where they had pinched the beer, and there were the cars outside the hotel, and there was the shadow of the Kirk where Charlie and his pal . . .

"Mr. MacTaggart—I was verra much surprised at such conduct in a son of yours."

"So was I," Geordie said. Constable Grigg had been some kind of a desk policeman all his service until he came to Drumfechan two years ago, and he was not too popular, having a knack of saying things a policeman need not say, and putting folks' backs up, and putting them higher if they were up already.

"In my opeenion, the law should have taken its course. Those were criminal offences. But due to influence being brought to bear, the offenders went scot free."

Six on the backside from Geordie MacTaggart was not quite scot free. But the stuck-up constable was right. Over there the men had begun to sing. One of them was leading in a song that Geordie remembered from long ago, from the ship that took him across the Atlantic for the Olympic Games at Boston. It was a lively French song called "Alouette."

There's no harm to them, he thought, a better thought in the darkness of his mood. Strangers from Scotland and Ireland and Europe too, and which of us has made them feel at home? But if they were all the likes of that McClintock, or of the one they called Cooligan and what he said to Jean, who would be anxious to make them feel at home? ". . . What was yon you said?" Geordie said to Constable Grigg, not a man he was too fond of.

"I said I hope your son will mend his ways before it is too late. If I may offer a word, Mr. MacTaggart, he would do well to take you as an example for his general behaviour."

The singing was louder, and more men gathered. "I see the mist is thinning. You're a good weather prophet, Mr. MacTaggart. Well now, I must be riding along. There are complaints that a collie dog of James Gordon's has been killing sheep, a serious business."

Geordie could have told the constable that on pay night Jimmy Gordon was more likely to be in the pub a hundred yards from here than at home two miles along the loch, but he did not feel like spoiling the constable's excuse. They had finished a last long chorus of "Alouette." The men were restless under the lamp. They milled about, and a couple squared off to one another, sparring. "Ta-ta then, Officer," Geordie said. "Watch out for motor-bikes."

He started his before the constable could more than frown at what might be an impertinence to the law from a law-abiding citizen who had recently been cautioned. Geordie stopped outside the bar, and pulled the heavy machine back on to its stand. The men were not moving now. They all faced along this way.

The public bar was nearly full, not crowded. The locals sat at the far end along the wall. They were the steadies; you wouldn't need to look to know who they would be on a Friday night. At this end were the Hydro boys, standing and sitting. The middle of the bar was empty, like a no-man's-land, and Geordie took the vacant stool. It creaked, and the legs were none too sound; he knew from experience in judging what could and could not take his weight; so he put one foot to the floor to ease its burden. "Well, if it isn't oor Geordie, a rare surprise."

"Hallo, Alec," he said to Alec Chisholm, and he nodded to the others, who included Jimmy Gordon. It was hot in here, and the smoke like blue mist. "A double Bell's," he said. "What'll you have, Jock?"

"A single, thanks, Geordie." Jock Burrell poured the double and the single drinks. He was a slow-spoken man with the complexion of the trade, his words and his drams under measured control.

"Here's tae us," Geordie said.

"Wha's like us," said Jock Burrell.

"Damn' few," Geordie said.

"They're a' deid," said Jock Burrell.

"May the Lord be thankit," Geordie said.

He held out for more. "On the house," Jock said. He had taken one small sip from his. Geordie's dad used to say that Bell's Perth Whisky was the best, and what Dad said was good enough. The taste of the best was not just to Geordie's taste, but the feeling was good when it got down to his midriff. He drank a glass of water for dilution.

"Awkward, eh, Geordie, the mischief our laddies was in."

"Aye, awkward," Geordie said. "But mischief's no' the right wor l for it."

"They were lucky. Was it the Laird got them off?"

"The Laird got them off; and you and the Minister let them off."

"What else could I do?"

"Aye, what could you do, that's right enough, Jock."

"Did you punish your Charlie?"

"Aye, I took the stick to him. Did you?"

"No," Jock said. "I'm no' muckle Geordie, I didna' dare. Tam's seventeen past, and stronger'n his dad. It would be me who would be getting the stick, and a heart attack thrown in." He laughed and Geordie laughed; and then Jock went away to serve the Hydro boys. Some took beer and some took rum.

Jock came back to mutter as he wiped the counter: "I heard one of them say: *Tell Cooligan he's here.* Would that be you they're meaning, Geordie?"

"It just might be," Geordie said. "What happened to your mirror?"

The long mirror behind Jock's row of bottles was

E

broken, smashed to starred smithereens in several places. "Mugs happened to it last Saturday nicht."

"Do you have insurance?"

"Aye, but what's insurance? What's insurance when folk are feared to come in, or feared to stay. Why couldn't our ane folk have a pint in peace?"

"That's right," Geordie said. The Drumfechan men were slipping out one by one. "Bell's, Jock," he said.

Jock served him. "It's the first time you ever set foot in here," he said. "It's real good to see you, Geordie, in mair ways than one. Mebbe they'll think twice the nicht."

"Mebbe not," Geordie said. "I'd thin out your sodgers, Jock, in case."

"Good idea," Jock said. He took away half the bottles from the row in front of the broken mirror. The Hydro boys were singing "Mademoiselle from Armentières." "Do you ken this Cooligan?"

"No," Geordie said. "I've heard tell of him. What's special about Cooligan?"

"He's top o' the peckin' order. Used to box heavy-weight professional, they say. I wouldn't be surprised."

"Is that so?" Geordie said. He was feeling fine, he was feeling just perfect. "What's that, Jock?"

"I says: the Hydro boys are watching you. Do they have it in for you some way?"

"That's possible. I caught a McClintock poaching this afternoon."

"*McClintock?* He's the bad one. Cooligan's just a bully-boy. But McClintock, he'd dig a knife in your back. Watch out for him."

"He's nursin' sair lugs the noo," Geordie said. "Or my name's not George MacTaggart."

Jock Burrell had a high cackle of a laugh, quite like the Laird's. "Man, Geordie," he said, "it's grand to see ye on the warpath, and you sae respectable, I didna ken you had it in ye."

"I'm no' on the warpath," Geordie said. "Far from it. I'm the Sleeping Beauty o' Sleepy Hollow. Gie us another yin, Jock."

"That's six doubles, Geordie."

"I said another yin, Jock."

"Aye, Geordie."

The door opened again. Every time it was pushed wide and then swung back before the spring to close, you could feel the movement of the air, a hint of freshness in the smoky fug. Why would folk waste their time in a place like this? "Yon's Cooligan."

Geordie did not look round at the famous Cooligan. He watched in the undamaged corner of the mirror. The man stood in the doorway, one hand on the door, and there were other men behind him. He was a big fair-haired chap in a red and black flannel shirt, open at the neck. He looked once along the room, slowly along and back, and his eyes stopped a second on Geordie in the mirror, moved on; and then he strolled to take a seat. He did not have the cocky bully-boy look about him that Geordie had expected. He just looked calm and sure of himself. "The usual, Jock," he said.

Demerara Rum, a spoonful of sugar, a slice of lemon, the spoon in the glass, filled from the kettle. Jock took it along to the end of the bar. Then there were more orders. Geordie had water with his Bell's

this time, half and half, it wasn't fiery in his throat.
He felt no different from the whisky. A slow thrum
in his head, but that wasn't whisky; it started when
he clipped McClintock, or before that even. What
for would folk want to drink the stuff, he thought.
Careful now. That's me being perfect. Geordie
chuckled.

"What's the joke, Geordie?"

"Perfection," he said. What was it? *"Perfection
personified*, that's the wee joke, that's the jokey,
Jocky boy." He spoke loudly enough for his voice
to carry, and the room was quiet.

"Here's Cooligan," Jock Burrell muttered.

Geordie looked at his glass and sipped from it and
put it down and picked it up and finished it.

"Would you be MacTaggart?"

The stool creaked as Geordie turned. The man
stood a few feet away, hands loose at his sides. He
was a good-looking chap, not pug-faced, not cauli-
flower-eared. He smiled a little. He was a tough one
all right. "I would," Geordie said. "Who would
you be?"

"Cooligan's the name," he said. "You hit one of
our boys the day."

"I did," Geordie said. "A couple of wee slaps I
gave him."

"And put him to the doctor. What for would you
hit a chap not half your size?"

"That's my business," Geordie said. "Ask him, or
mind your own."

Cooligan did not move, hands still loose at his sides
still smiling. He was a big man, not so tall, not nearly

so heavy as Geordie himself, and with a much shorter reach, but he would be quicker. He was a lot younger too, mebbe thirty or so. He looked at Geordie's left cheek. "Did she scratch ye?" he said.

Geordie turned. "A dram, Jock," he said, and turned back. "Say what you said . . ." he began, but the stool buckled under him. The legs folded, collapsed instantly to dump Geordie on his backside on the floor, and all the men laughed, they all laughed their heads off except Cooligan.

"You're drunk," he said. "I'm no' wastin' ma time on drunks." He turned away.

Geordie was not drunk. He was cold sober after whatever it was that he had drunk, and he was on his feet and he picked up the remains of that damned stool and he threw it across the room to hit the wall, to smash the framed verse by Rabbie Burns: *John Anderson, my jo John, when we were first acquent*, and Geordie's jacket was off, and he was cold sober and, click, red click in his head, he was fighting mad. It's a new feeling, he had time to think. "Drunk, did ye say?" he said. "Come and find out."

Cooligan came. He came lightly in the boxer's crouch, weight forward, chin tucked below his right hand, leading with his left; prod, prod, prod, and Geordie let loose a right. Cooligan took it on his shoulder, and Geordie never saw the fist come over, a right hook to his eye. It was a real professional's punch, short, timed right. Geordie shook the dizziness from his head. He closed with Cooligan, used his greater weight to crowd him back, keep crowding. Another one of those, on the jaw it would be the next time, and Geordie would be out cold. Cooligan was fighting fair. Fight fair and be knocked out? To hell with it.

Geordie's head was clear again in the clinch. Quick now! *One, two—one*: take the neck of his shirt in your left hand, thrust him off, hold him off, well beyond his reach, shake him, shake him one-handed to rattle the teeth in his head, shake him silly. Now: *two*: Geordie did not clench his fist. He hit Cooligan with all his strength with the palm, with the base of his open hand on the side of the jaw. He changed hands and gave it to him the other way, and that was Cooligan. Geordie laid him down gently to sleep on the floor. "Who's next?" he said. But they all went out. They backed out, but he did not follow. Something crashed outside.

"Man!" Jock Burrell said, "I never seen the like." He looked at Geordie in some wonder.

"It was dirrty," Geordie said. "I'm not just too sorry, though." He picked up Cooligan in his arms, laid him on the bench, and put his own jacket for a pillow. Cooligan slept on.

"Here!" said Jock. "Hold it to yer eye." It was raw meat, cooling the fire round Geordie's eye. What with the monkey-puzzle scratches and that eye closed tight already, the left side of his face would not be just too bonny.

Jock went and locked the door and left the key in it. "A minute's peace for a change," he said. "A dram, Geordie—one for the road?"

"I don't mind," Geordie said. What's this I'm doing? he thought. Drinking, when I can't be bothered with the stuff. Fighting, hitting two men when I haven't laid hands on a chap since I was bantam

Geordie at the school. Jock had locked the door for a minute's peace for a change, but it was not peace that Geordie wanted. A siren sounded far away. It rose to a wail, and held it a few seconds, and died down. He drank his dram.

"Yon's the sireen at the dam," Jock said. "What for would that be blowing?"

Cooligan slept on the bench. He was pale, except round the jaws, but his breathing was steady. "Mebbe we should revive him, Jock."

"Och, leave him be. Bring him round too quick, and he'll come out fighting."

"A wet clout, Jock."

Geordie wiped his face with the cold wet cloth, and Cooligan stirred. He sighed, shook his head, and sat up straight. Mebbe Jock had been right . . . "Was it the open hand you hit me with?"

"Aye," Geordie said.

"A Clydesdale couldna' kick like yon." Cooligan started to laugh, but put his head in his hands. "Sufferin' Moses," he said.

Hammering at the door. "Mr. MacTaggart! Mr. MacTaggart!" It was a girl's voice, loud and excited.

Geordie went to the door. "What is it, Maggie?"

"I saw the men run from here and across the brig, so I got on my bike and went after them, and then the siren sounded. They're coming, Mr. MacTaggart. There's fifty of them coming after you. You'll not stand a chance. Get away quick!" Maggie Oliphant was out of breath again. She was a good fat pal of his, and she had had a long hard day of it, and now worry made near-hollows in her cheeks.

"Thanks, Maggie," he said. "Give Cooligan a dram, Jock. I'll square up later."

Geordie went out. They had tipped his bike up, and in the cold air there was a whiff of petrol. There were people in the Square, all Drumfechan people. They stood quite still, and none of them spoke. The nip of the night was a grand refreshment. He could run a mile, or two, or five, and leave Charlie the runner far behind. That was the feeling Geordie had. But it was only a sprint to the Roman Brig, to crouch at the curve of the low parapet, to listen to them coming, and they were nearly here. Faithful Maggie was right, a lot of men out for trouble.

It was an ancient bridge from Roman times, barely wide enough to take one car. It went in a single arch over the River Fechan, which was not too deep at the Roman Brig and not too shallow and not too fast, a grand place to watch the salmon run on their way to the loch, to the spawning beds beyond the loch.

Now their feet sounded hollow on the brig. Geordie still waited. He bided his time. Now!

He ran to meet them. It was quite dark, but the stars were out and there was the lamp not far behind him and to the side. They can't see me too well, he thought. But he could see them, a jostling crowd, two or three abreast, and some had sticks, and was that gleam a spanner?

He knew just what to do. He bent low like a rugger forward to make a twenty-two-stone battering ram of himself to split them down the middle. The first few ranks never knew what hit them until they were toppling left and right over the parapet into the cold November water of the River Fechan.

That was ten, eleven, twelve, a sweep to the right, a sweep to the left, and over they went.

Then he met a solid mass at the top of the arch, and he could not penetrate, so he had to take them one by one. They were forcing him back now, he had to yield, taking blows on his arms, and one thump with something hard on his head, dizzy again, but shake it off, pick this one up and throw him, not topple him, a grand splash he made. "Take that from Sleepy Hollow." Twenty-one, twenty-two, twenty-three chaps floundering in four feet of water. But then they came no more. They turned and ran back over the bridge with Geordie after them. He caught a last one, and him he pushed in, and that was that.

Geordie stood in the middle of the Roman Brig, hands on his hips. He was very tired, and the bridge heaved up at him now suddenly, and those softies were feared to come at him again, and he wasn't finished yet.

"Will you come quietly?" It was the voice of that policeman.

"Och awa'," Geordie said. "Dinna' spoil my fun." He swayed on his feet. He felt queer now, just muzzy a bit from all his exertions in the cold night air.

"Disturbing the peace, assault, drunkenness too. You're under arrest."

"Go to hell," Geordie said, still watching his enemies who lurked across the bridge.

The truncheon clapped like an explosion on Geordie's head. It was not enough and just a bit too much. He turned on that policeman, spun him round, took him by the collar and the breeks, and dumped him into the River Fechan. Geordie leaned over the parapet. Constable Grigg floundered a bit, and got to his feet. The policeman's cap was floating away to join the North Sea.

"Oh, I say, George!"

"Steady now, Geordie! Easy does it."

"Easy does what?" he said, and the Minister giggled. They each took an arm. The Laird and the Minister had arrested him, but he could not throw them off without, without what? Without pushing them into pneumonia at their time of life. So Geordie suffered himself to be led back to Drumfechan Square. His escort were not too steady on their pins, poor old chaps, they kept making him blunder this way and that. "Aim for the bull's-eye, George," said the Laird.

"What bullsh-eye?" Geordie inquired. He remembered thinking something about a bull's-eye when fat Maggie spat a champion jet.

"Police Station bull's-eye, George." The Laird began to laugh again. With him and the Minister and other daft folk laughing and a cheer or two, Geordie's anger was redder, still redder.

"Hud yer whissht!" he growled at the world about him. Silence fell.

Who was this? This was some chap he hit some time or other. Och aye, it was Cooligan.

"Man," Cooligan said, "yon was the brawest sicht I ever did see in a' my born days."

Now *Perthshire Constabulary* above the door. "He's coming," hissed the Laird. "The law drips wetly at our heels. Don't worry, George. I'll get you off in no time flat."

"The Laird'll do no shuch shing. Did the Laird hear me?"

"Yes, yes, George."

"But, Geordie . . . !"

"Och, hud yer whissht!" Geordie said again. It was no way to speak to a minister, but Geordie was not exactly caring.

The kettle that was Geordie's rage had taken a long time coming to the boil, and it kept on boiling. It boiled all Saturday and Sunday in the lock-up, and boiled right over at the County Court on Monday morning when they tried to take pictures of him, but he soon settled that. He pleaded guilty to every charge —drunkenness, disturbing the peace, assault, although that policeman had not laid the most serious complaint. "Why am I not charged with assaulting the law in uniform on duty or the like of that?" he thundered in the court.

The magistrate frowned, biting his lip in worried vexation. "Because you didn't, I suppose," he said, "or the like of that." Then the magistrate coughed, smashing down his gavel, and it was his turn to thunder: "Silence in the court!"

Geordie glared about the hushed place, and there in a corner he saw poor Jean, dabbing a handkerchief to her tears. She would not look at him.

Exemplary record—some provocation—plea of guilty, no alternative but five pounds or seven days— but the Court had already been informed that a fine would be paid.

"No, it won't," Geordie said. So he went to gaol for seven days, less time awaiting trial.

They were pretty decent to him. On Tuesday they

brought a bundle of newspapers. "Front page in them all, Geordie, it's a smasher, you should read it."

"No," he said. "Thanks just the same." He couldn't help it that he had been a well-known figure long ago, and now in the news again as a disgrace.

"A visitor to see ye, Geordie."

"I tellt ye—no visitors."

The food was not too terrible, even after Jean's grand cooking, but he had a prisoner's hunger. "Here's double rations, Geordie," they said on the Wednesday.

"One man, one ration," he said, wanting no favours.

"Och, come on now, Geordie. You've twice the frame to fill. We're no' wantin' you to waste away. We're no' wantin' a bad reputation."

Geordie repeated his refusal, but politely. The kettle of his rage had stopped boiling. It simmered down. It was cooling quickly.

He saw now that by going to prison he had not shown anyone, proved anything. By going to prison he had made things worse. And what would Jean say to a drunken gaolbird of a husband? Geordie knew.

Now his angry grunts gave way to groans of remorse. Now, in the solitary hours, he went over all his sins—the example he had set to Charlie less than a week after giving him a hiding, hitting wee men, fighting dirty, throwing the constable in the river, bringing shame upon the glen. He had no alternative —come Friday night, he would give in his notice, to spare the old Laird from giving it to him. He remembered the Laird and the Minister arresting him and leading him between them, but after that he could not remember anything, lost in drunkenness. It was a sore disgrace.

By Friday his black eye was going yellow at the edges, the monkey-puzzle wounds had nearly healed, and his other bruises were better too. "Home again, Geordie, eh?" said the driver of McCrimmon's bus, with a decent kind of a laugh, sheepish about Geordie being out of gaol, and the shameful behaviour, and the black eye too.

"H'mm," Geordie said, and paid his fare and went to the back of the empty bus. He looked out of the window. It was a nice November afternoon. The sun was pale, but it laid a bonny green colour on the kale, and there was a covey of partridges on the stubble, and three cock pheasants near the wood. *Three cock pheasants?*

But to-morrow . . . The morn's morn was the Laird's first pheasant shoot, and he had forgotten all about it, and through prideful anger he had refused to pay a fine when he could have done his work, finding beaters, putting place-sticks for the guns, a hundred things. That settles it, Geordie thought. A kind of sad tranquillity came over him, saying hallo again and soon to be good-bye as McCrimmon's bus wound up the glen, the peaceful glen where he had lived his life until he shattered the peace of that glen.

That settles it. I'll make a new start some place where nobody knows my reputation. How would Canada do? They must have grand big estates in Canada needing to be keepered by an experienced man without references. Or here's another idea, would I join the Mounties in the frozen North? No, too old for the Mounties at forty-three. Or here's another —some real James Bond might be wanting a body-guard.

Geordie's imagination, always vivid, took him off on strange adventures with some real James Bond, chasing, rescuing, enduring unmentionable tortures from the wicked blonde, bruised and battered but free again to fight against terrific odds . . .

"Here we are, Geordie."

That brought him back to earth from the fighting that could become like an enjoyable vice. "Thanks," he said, getting down from the bus. He had dismounted from McCrimmon's bus so many times, so many ordinary times; and one great time when he was home from winning at the Olympic Games, and there was trouble even then because Jean had heard false stories about him and Helga Sorensen, the Lady Shot-putter; and one bad time, which was now this afternoon, and Jean would be waiting in the house, and what would Jean be saying?

But the cottage was empty. The dogs were barking up at the kennels. I'll go and see them in a minute, Geordie thought. The dogs don't know better than to bark a welcome to me.

There was a sheet of paper on the kitchen table. *Gone to Drumfechan. See Laird's letter, Jean.* The letter was underneath. On the envelope: *Mr. G. MacT.* This'll be my notice, Geordie thought, and he opened it.

"Geo.,
Pl. come qu. cel. opt. prior."

and the Laird's initials underneath. *Qu. cel. opt. prior,* whatever it meant, was *as quickly as possible, top priority,* in the Laird's code language for time-saving and efficiency. So Geordie put on his best suit of Drum-fechan tweed, the one he wore on shooting days, like to-morrow would have been, and he set off for the Big House to be sacked by the Laird in person with puffing of cheeks and daft asides. Get it over with. But he stopped to say hallo to the Labradors—Bess, Toby and Sheena. Their tails wagged their bodies, so pleased to see him.

Geordie walked on, between dark yews and smooth old beeches, past that monkey-puzzle; and he was thinking that he would have to run the gauntlet of his mother, so to speak, and he would make it short and manly, the way an apology should be. He would say: *I'm right sorry, Mum, for what I did*.

But there was nobody in the kitchen end of the Big House. He went through cold stone passages to the Laird's study, where he knocked.

"Hallo, George, just the chap I want. Look, George, be a sport and change jobs, would you? This is what we need . . ."

Change jobs? Not be sacked outright? To be a labourer? No, it was to be a forester, a very low profession. I'll not do it, Geordie thought.

"Are you deaf, man? What we need are small pine branches, two or three feet long, y'know, plenty of greenery. And holly with berries—I realise it isn't Christmas time, but festive time, that's good enough. And some yew, better get some yew. Take the Land-Rover. No, too late now. Do it in the morning. Oh, and I say, we could use some beech with the brown leaves still on, very pretty, reminds me of that sonnet and myself." The Laird was at the window, looking out. He had hardly glanced at Geordie. The Laird was in a great state of excitement. "Now what else? Oh yes. Rhododendrons are a good glossy green, a few bits of the common old Ponticum, not my special pets, of course. Got all that, George?"

"What's it for, sir?" Geordie said.

"But I told you, idiot." The Laird turned and stared at idiot Geordie's damaged eye. "H'mm," he said. "A champion shiner, a bit past its best. For the dance, George."

"What dance is the Laird meaning?"

"At the Parish Hall to-morrow night. Everyone knows about it. Oh, but you've been away, though, haven't you? We're entertaining the Hydro chaps, and your job is outdoor decoration; the women are doing the paper stuff, the coloured festoonery, supper tables too, they're on that now. And I'll tell you a stroke of genius I had. Those Hydro types are a bit starved for . . . er, for what it takes, so I've fixed that with the Hydropathic—hydroelectric and hydropathic, kissing cousins by the Roman Brig, eh, George. Well, to make a long story short, two busloads of Hydropathic belles are honouring us."

The Hydropathic was a sanitorium place where people from all over came for cures, and there was a big staff.

". . . The water treatment, George, most efficacious as you ought to know. Well anyway, Jean—and your mother too—they've been the most wonderful help to me about the whole thing. I think Jean feels sorry for those chaps, a little guilty perhaps, as do we all."

And if Jean felt sorry for those chaps, and guilty about those chaps, what did Jean feel about her husband, Geordie? And that Cooligan?

F

"You look so glumly at me, man. Don't you know who brought this miracle about?"

Yes, it seemed that the Laird had achieved a miracle. But he was so daft to-day, jumping about from this to the next thing, that Geordie's head was in a whirling muddle.

"Well, now I have a thousand things to do, but we must have a long talk sometime about your sins. Oh, and you won't forget that greenery to-morrow morning?"

"To-morrow was to have been the Laird's first pheasant shoot."

"Was it? Oh, my God, I'd quite forgotten. Let's cancel it."

"We'll need to," Geordie said, and drew breath to make one first apology, but the Laird was off again:

"But we can't cancel. I've asked all the guns. My name would be even worse Perthshire mud than it is already."

"I have no beaters. The Laird kens fine what it is to get beaters."

"Beaters? Beaters? I can soon fix that." The Laird darted to the telephone. ". . . 216, I said, gel. Drumfechan Hydro? Mr. Cooligan, please. He's on the *Euclid*? Get him off it, then. Yes, I'll hang on." The Laird covered the mouthpiece. "Poor fella's doing geometry, high standard they expect these days, cruelty to ex-prize-fighters, I would say. Talking of which, George, how did you enjoy your week's retreat, find time to ponder your many crimes?—— Oh, hallo, Cooligan, Sleepy Hollow here. Look, we need fifteen beaters for a pheasant shoot to-morrow morning, eight forty-five, old clothes, usual rates. You can?"

The Laird hung up. "That's that," he said, pleased with himself. "Beaters are easy, George, if you have the right contacts at Tammany Hall."

"There's no place sticks for the guns."

"Not essential. You and I can tell them where to stand." He darted an anxious glance at Geordie. "You seem down in the dumps, George. After all you've done, you should be trying to look at the brighter side."

"Yessir," Geordie said. You should try, but trying was not always succeeding. "What about the Laird's decorations?"

"Yes, that's a point. Oh, I have it—another easy one—young Charles could do that. I fancy he could drive the Land-Rover round the estate to pick up greenery, eh, George?"

"I fancy he could," Geordie said. "If the Laird was to ask him."

"You ask him. A grand boy, that. He'll jump to your command, or I'm a Dutchman."

The Laird's to be a Dutchman, *then*, Geordie nearly said, but he said: "If the Laird has no more, I'll be . . ."

"Yes, yes, George, see you at the crack of dawn."

In this mood of the Laird's it was hopeless to say anything to him. "Good night, sir," Geordie said, and turned.

"What about that for a likeness, George?"

It was a framed photograph above the door, a big one, about two feet by one and a half, and it was a picture of Geordie outside the County Court last Monday when they wanted to photograph him and he was forbidding it. He looked a good deal larger than life between two small policemen, and his fists were clenched and his hands were raised, and the black eye was closed, and he was snarling. It was a painful shock, it was frightening to Geordie to see the man-gorilla that was him, the real wicked killer him . . .

"It was in the Scottish *Daily Press*, and y'know what I think of *them*, George; but I buried my pride and telephoned, and there you are, I must say it was pretty civil of them to rally round with a colossal glossy with the editor's compliments. Whenever I have a particularly sticky interview in this room, and God knows I have plenty, and things become acrimonious, as they invariably do, I shall gently turn the chap round to face the door, and I shall say: *I very much look forward to introducing you to my gamekeeper.*"

Geordie escaped the Laird's daft laughter. It was not yet quite dark, but darkness gathered. Even if the Laird would keep him on, and it seemed as if he might, *we must have a long talk some time about your sins.* Even so, how could he face the shame of it, face the black rage of himself every time he turned to face that door? Face the shame that was his, the shame that he alone had brought upon the glen to make everyone feel guilty about the Hydro chaps, feel sorry for what Geordie MacTaggart did, have a dance to make up for it. And now they would all be friends, and who would be the outcast, deserving it, reminded of it every day, a disgrace to his wife and son? He would hand in his notice to-morrow night.

Geordie gave the monkey-puzzle a wide berth, going home to face the music. Lights were on in the cottage, and sounds of wood-splitting from the scullery. That would be Charlie scowling at his chores. I ken fine now where he got the scowl from, Geordie thought.

"Dad! Man, Dad, it's grand to see you." Charlie jumped up and he did a caper, a light-footed unthinking dance of joy, and his eyes were bright like they used to be. And then he stood still and stared at his father, as if he had never seen George MacTaggart before. "I was just home when we heard the siren, so we thought it might be a fire or something, so Mum said okay, I could go. Then she said: *Hang on. I have a wee hunch. I'm coming too*, and we got on our bikes, and we just got there in time to see you charge them at the Roman Brig, like ninepins right and left, and then . . ." Charlie bent over, smacking knees and shaking head, his laughter was wild. "And then yon constable. Man, Dad, you were perfect!"

"But, Charlie, I was the worse for drink."

"Och, Dad, you're havering. Whoever heard tell of a man the worse for drink throwing twenty-five tough cookies off a bridge. And anyway . . ."

"And anyway?"

Now running feet, and it was Jean, and she threw herself, just took a jump to throw herself into Geordie's arms. "My big bad laddie, I'm sae proud of you." She was half crying with laughter in his arms. It was all a strange surprise to him.

"Have you seen the papers, Dad?"

"No," he said. It was a warm strange feeling of surprise. Charlie had put the clippings in an album, which even had a title on the cover, painted white: GEORDIE AT THE BRIG.

And talk about newspaper blether: . . . *the great Geordie wins again . . . triumphs against fearful odds . . . forces unconditional surrender . . . defeated enemy offer to pay reparations in shape of fine, but raging Mac-Taggart elects durance vile.* So it was the Hydro chaps, that was decent of them. . . . *Court quails when Sir Geordie Horatius Galahad demands why graver charges not preferred against him . . .*

"The Laird soon fixed that," Jean said. "I heard him. The Laird says to the pollisman: *M'dear fella, any cop who testified to breaking his truncheon over the Lusty Champion of Drumfechan's cranium would be a laughing stock, dripping wet at that. You have been warned.*" Jean could copy the Laird's clipped la-di-da just right.

Supper was a feast to celebrate the prodigal father's return. It was tender stew with the dark brown gravy that only Jean could make, it was floury potatoes and brussels sprouts. It was Jean's own meringues and dollops of thick cream, too grand a feast for much conversation. Geordie tucked in with an ex-prisoner's appetite. Jean giggled once for no reason at all, and that set Charlie into laughter too.

"What's the joke?" Geordie growled. He knew that he was the joke, and he knew that he had them guessing too, not quite sure about that wicked temper. Geordie was none too pleased or proud of himself for what he had done, but he was happy, he was very happy. So he growled again to keep them guessing. But Jean and Charlie laughed all the more, like a pair of bairns.

After supper he told Charlie about the Laird's greenery.

"Okay, Dad." He was keen. So the Laird was right. The Laird was no Dutchman.

Then Charlie went out, and in a minute or two there came a squeal, a spank, a plaintive wail. "The pipes!" Geordie said in wonderment.

"He's been practising all week," Jean smiled, watching Geordie.

It was a grand selection, ending with the wildest, brawest tune of all, "Highland Laddie." Geordie was happy, feeling the tingle of "Highland Laddie."

And so to bed. Now Jean slept beside him, and Geordie was thinking. He was thinking about what his mum used to say to him that the only reward of virtue was virtue, the saying went. So it stood to reason that the only reward of vice should be vice. Yet it seemed in one case anyway in this daft world that the only reward of vice was virtue. Too complicated, he was getting sleepy. And then suddenly he heard Charlie's eager voice: *Man, Dad, you were perfect.*

Geordie laughed. He shook in silent laughter, not to waken Jean, but she woke up. "My wee Geordie," she said in the darkness of the night. "Big bad laddie, what's the joke?"

"Och, nothing," he said. And soon they slept.

Interval

"Laird," Bridget said, which meant that she wished to go and see him; and if Geordie did not yield there would be howls from Miss MacTaggart on his back.

"Hail, George. Greetings, Fair Papoose. Have a Curiously Strong." The Laird dipped into his pocket for a peppermint. "What's new, George?"

"Nothing much, sir."

"You're telling me there's nothing much." The Laird was at his tree nursery, a fenced-in place with rows and rows of seedlings. "See my New World prizes!" He pointed at a row apart. "Dug from the forest primeval, smuggled by jet in a plastic bag to flourish in this alien soil. A miracle, I say. *Betula Papyrifera*, *Abies balsamis*, *Acer sacc* . . . All thanks to our man in New Brunswick."

"Baby trees," Bridget said. "What's trees?"

"*What's trees?* A searching question, what indeed are trees? You tell the young lady, George."

"Trees are things God makes to grow."

"That's fixed her," said the Laird, delighted.

"What's God?"

"God is trees too," Geordie said, which seemed to fix her.

"A master of the equivocal absolute, George Mac-Taggart, S.J." The Laird chuckled a bit. "Mighty of stature, deep as a well. But much as I admire you, George, I find you boring. I find everything boring in this place, not least myself. Oh, for the good old days. Talking of which, what news of Charles?"

"The last we heard was from Edmonton, and he was just flying north, to the bush, he called it, to near some Lake Athabaska for the summer."

"Athabaska, ah Athabaska, Athabaska."

"And who does the Laird think Charlie met up with in Edmonton? Yon Cooligan. He was down for the week-end from building some dam in the Rocky Mountains."

"Cooligan and Charles—poor scarlet Edmonton. What wouldn't I give . . . But here I am, condemned in my dotage to this backwater."

"The Laird used to complain enough when the Hydro Scheme first started."

"Well, I learned better. I learned a bit about the spice of life. All gone, not even Charles to make things bearable."

The truth was that as Charlie grew up, he and the Laird became a bad influence on one another—any daft scheme of the Laird's, and Charlie would put his brains to it, like the time . . .

"You're bored, George, too. I can tell it in your grumpy-grumphs. No more battles at the Roman Brig. How long ago was that?"

"Three years come November, it would be," Geordie said.

"Ah well, Miss Bridget makes one lively addition, that I will admit. Mending butts, is that the order of the day'"

"Yessir," Geordie said.

"May I stroll along?" His stroll used to be at five miles an hour, tireless on those lanky legs. All Geordie's life the Laird had seemed old to him, the same ageless age. But now his body lagged from the pace of his mind. "They go away," he said. "The best ones leave us, and just as well. I can't see young Charles confined in this glen. Even Canada may have to look to her seams, eh, George?"

"That's right, sir," Geordie said. Charlie had passed top in first-year forestry at the University of New Brunswick, and he was getting a scholarship, and he was earning good money in the woods this summer. He was doing just fine, except that from what Geordie's Cousin Elspeth in Toronto did not quite say, Charlie's visit at Christmas had livened that city up a bit. ". . . What, sir?"

"I said the Oliphant gel is due home on a flying visit—some job escorting a child to England. I wonder how many airline seats are charged for in such a case, tut-tut, not worthy of me. Well, I shall retrace my steps. Good-bye, then, George. Farewell, Lady Bridget. I might see you later on. Here, have one for the hill road."

"Ta-ta, Laird," she said, and Geordie walked on. He carried his daughter in her grandfather's pack from Black Watch days. He had made a frame in it, and Bridget sat in comfort, Queen of the Castle. "Love Laird," she said. It was not only peppermint love. *She's fair daft about men*, Jean said. *Too young to know the truth, poor bairn.*

"Hold on tight," Geordie said when he climbed the wall by the hill gate, remembering—always something to remember at forty-six—that it was here he had found the wool from Charlie's green jersey to catch Charlie lying.

The morning was fine, a few white ships of cloud were sailing, shadow and sunshine on the hill. With the crying of the sheep, and the calling of the grouse, and the murmur of the wind so warm and kind, and Bridget riding pillion seat for company, you should not wish for more. Yet Geordie was not contented in his mind. *They go away*, the old Laird said. *The best ones leave us, and just as well.* And who do they leave behind?

I'll feel better when I get working, Geordie thought, and he turned off the hill road to follow the line of butts up the shoulder of the West Tully. Start from the top and work back down. There was just tidying and turfing to be done. Although I say it myself, he thought. My grouse butts are grouse butts.

He put Bridget down, and kicked about the heather to make sure there were no adders—very rare at Drumfechan, but still. She played a bit, and talked to herself a bit and to him a bit while he mended that top butt. Then they started down the line.

"Bird," she said, before he had seen the eagle. It was far away, soaring above the corrie where they had nested ever since Geordie could remember. Eagles were protected by law, and by the Laird, who wanted to have grouse and eagles both. "Story," she said.

It was an old story about the day when Geordie and Jean climbed to the eagle's nest, and he had tried first, but he could not reach, strain as he might, he could not reach the ledge. So it was taller Jean who saw the eagle chicks.

Bridget laughed heartily. "Big mummy, wee

daddy." It was very funny, and so it was, and that same day Geordie had written away for Henry Samson's course in physical development. All those years to make yourself big when probably God had decided anyway that you would be a muckle lump. Vanity, vanity. Geordie laughed now too. He felt better with the comfort of the work.

The morning wore on to sandwich time, and they were back beside the road where a hill burn splashed its way. It had been a dry summer so far, a good year for the hatching and the growing of the grouse. All the seasons stretching back, the great ones and the disastrous ones, the dry ones and the wet ones, with grouse disease and the Laird's beloved eagles, same trials and blessings, getting older.

In Charlie's last letter—he wrote once a month, or less than that, but they were worth waiting for, he had a great way of taking you with him to where he was—Charlie wrote: *I think the only real people are the ones who stay at home.* It was a good thing for him to write to his father and his mother.

Bridget ate her peanut butter sandwich, her grannie's shortbread and half a banana, and she drank her milk. She was like Jean to look at, and she was a pocketful of pep. Now Geordie rinsed out her mug, and she made shapes with it from the sand beside the burn. Soon it would be time to move to another line of butts. Geordie closed his eyes for a five-minute nap.

"Man come." He was drifting into a nice small snooze of middle age, no business to have a baby daughter, grand company though, grand company. But she was shaking him. So Geordie sat up, fuzzy a moment, but he had not slept.

The man came down the hill road. He walked fast, with the easy stride of youth, and Geordie put the binoculars on to him. It was not a man, but a girl in a dark kilt or skirt and a pale red jersey and hair of a fair chestnut colour. She was a tall girl, carrying a knapsack. She would be a hiker, a stranger to these parts. Geordie put the small glasses back into his handkerchief pocket, pleased that a well set-up lassie swinging her kilt could not but exchange the time of day at a chance meeting on the hill.

She was nearly here. On close observation she was so grandly designed a stranger girl with long bare legs that Geordie picked Bridget up for him to have a diversion.

"Mr. MacTaggart!" She said his name, but he did not know her from Adam, or from Eve.

"Don't you know me?" she said, and she was blushing as she smiled, not offended that he should not know her. "Maggie," she said.

In Geordie's quiet life not too many surprises occurred, and the lack of them might have contributed to what the Laird called his grumphy-grumphs this morning, and here suddenly was a huge surprise, huge Maggie no longer huge, but fined down by some miracle to be just about the brawest muckle lassie that Geordie had ever observed. Well, you could have knocked him over with a feather. But he remembered his manners, and stood to shake hands with her, and he was not the taller by so much. "Maggie," he said. "It's grand to see you."

"Mr. MacTaggart! Och, it's just wonderful to meet you the first one of all. And this is Bridget?"

"So you heard we had Bridget?"

"Of course I heard."

"You're looking well," he said. "You're looking just fine." And so she was and he could not believe it. "So you walked from Altnadean?"

"I was early in Perth on the London train, and no bus to Drumfechan this forenoon. So I took the one to Altnadean. It's a fine day for a walk."

"Aye," he agreed, "a fine day for a walk." Ten miles would be just a stroll to Maggie now.

"Big lassie," Bridget said.

Maggie laughed and bent to lift her right up. "Wee lassie," she said, and set her down in the heather.

"More," Bridget said. Again the supple easy stoop and flow of body and arm, and Bridget was high above Maggie's head.

Geordie turned away to the valley of the Fechan and closed his eyes and saw the real Maggie, poor fat Maggie all bulges and chins. He turned back, but this one seemed real enough, with bright brown eyes and bonny fair hair, it used to be like tangled straw.

"It's good to be home," she said.

"Aye," he said. "There's no place like home."

"It's strange after all the other places to see the one real place." Which might be something like what Charlie wrote.

"Just a short visit, Maggie?"

"Five days," she said. "I had the chance to bring this wee boy—he lost his . . ." Maggie glanced at Bridget. "Well, it's a long story, but just five days."

"And your mum says you like New Zealand."

"I like it fine," she said, looking at him. "You're just the same," Maggie said. "I knew you would be, Mr. MacTaggart."

"Laird coming." The small red car climbed fast. It was the Laird's new toy, his beloved Mini, and he was a menace in it.

Now he stopped, switched off, and extracted himself leg by leg, then the rest of him. "Thought I would find you here," he said, and noticed Maggie and took off his bonnet. "Who? What goddess, this? Why? How? Can it be? But she is. Margaret, my dear child, what a sight for ancient eyes." So then there was a great re-union, and the Laird talked nineteen to the dozen, and he prowled round Maggie, paying daft compliments: ". . . Such form, such lissome grace. How did you do it, gel? Did you starve yourself to this perfection?"

"No," she said. "My appetite's just huge."

"And you never dropped a hint, not even to your parents?"

Maggie shook her head. She was not at all shy with the Laird of Drumfechan.

"Marvellous," said the Laird. "The whole glen will goggle while it eats its hat. She's a wow, George, isn't she?"

"Well, yes," Geordie said. What else could he say? And Maggie blushed.

"*Well, yes*, indeed. What a niggling understatement. And your academic achievements—at least you dropped us a hint of them. I hear you're the brightest co-ed in all New Zealand."

Maggie laughed again. "Home's just the same," she said. "And the Laird is the samest."

"Same old nincompoop," he said. "Well, hop into my souped-up Cooper, and let us give the glen a treat."

"Me come," Bridget said.

"May I take her, George?"

"If the Laird will drive slowly."

"Have a heart, George, dammit," the Laird said testily.

Maggie stowed the knapsack and took Bridget on her knee. "Cheerio, Mr. MacTaggart. Cheeribye for now."

"Cheeribye," he said. The Laird drove away like a snail, and Maggie Oliphant waved at the window, and Geordie went back to mending grouse butts. A few times that afternoon he closed his eyes and it was always dumpling Maggie that he saw. Once he saw her puffing and panting in her belly crawl.

"A grand figure of a lassie she's turned out to be," said Jean. "It's like a miracle, and her not spoilt a bit."

"Just the same Maggie," Geordie said.

"*Just the same Maggie.* That shows all you ken about a woman."

"I meant inside like," he said.

"So did I," she said. "Och, men!" At forty-five Jean was a mite plumper than before she had the baby, and more easy-going in her ways—still Jean, though.

Next day the weather was close, and the wireless forecast thunderstorms for the afternoon, so Geordie did not take Bridget with him. He was out early on the motor-bike, going past the back of the Big House, but his mother was waiting for him, as she often did when she heard the bike. Other people might feel ups and downs, but not Mum, so far as Geordie ever knew. She was the same shrewd easy-going body she had always been, and that made him her same small boy. "Off to the hill?" she said.

"Aye," he said. "I might get the butts done the day."

"Did you remember your waterproof?"

"No," he said. "I forgot my wee undies too."

"Geordie! Well, I must away in to cook the Laird's kedgeree. He's to meet Maggie Oliphant at nine for a walk round the place. The Laird says Maggie is the best miracle that's happened to Drumfechan since the loaves and fishes. A bonny warm-hearted lassie she's turned out to be, and cheery too with the daftest stories, and that's what the Laird needs, cheering up."

"The Laird needs a big warm cheery lassie, mebbe like auld King David stricken wi' the years."

"Geordie!" His mother shook with shocked laughter in almost as many places as Maggie Oliphant used to shake. And then she went in, and he rode on.

It was hot on the hill, so sweltering and still that Geordie took off his shirt and worked bare to the waist. He took twenty minutes off at dinner-time, then back to it as thunder muttered. There were no clouds to be seen, just a haze that thickened down in the north-west. Geordie worked on, with a grand sweat pouring off him in the sun. I'm as good at forty-six as ever I was, he thought, the last butt done by three o'clock, and thunder louder now, and the sky was indigo below the sun. Still plenty of time. He went down to a hill burn to splash himself in the good cold peaty water. Then he climbed again to the butt beyond the Lum.

G

"Hallo, Mr. MacTaggart." Up popped Maggie Oliphant from inside the butt.

"Hallo, Maggie," he said. Her appearance was no less surprising to him than yesterday.

"Dad's away this afternoon," she said. "So I said I would keep an eye on the sheep. And then I got a wee bit lost among all those hillocks near the junipers; and then I was lucky enough to catch a glimpse of you, and that put me on my road. Man, Mr. Mac-Taggart, you make grand butts." But she was staring at him, not the butt. Geordie felt awkward, him without a shirt. He put it on, and his jacket too.

The sun was gone, and thunder clouds had climbed the sky. There would be less time than he had thought. "We'll need to be quick," he said, but as he spoke a fork of lightning stabbed, and he counted to the thunder, twelve seconds, too close to have time to get to the motor-bike and down before the storm.

"Mebbe we should shelter at the Lum," Maggie said.

"Mebbe so," he said. She followed him to the Lum, fat faithful Maggie, but when he stood aside to let her in, she was not fat faithful Maggie, she was a stranger from New Zealand.

"It's nice and cosy, Mr. MacTaggart."

It was not just too cosy. It was damp, and the floor was wet and hard, but it was shelter from the rain, a real plout beyond the door, through which fat Maggie had spat her champion jet another time. "What's it like in New Zealand?" he asked the stranger.

"Well, Mr. MacTaggart . . ." and she talked about New Zealand, the friendly Maoris and the kind white people and the strange birds there were, and a grand climate except for wind, all the same things that he had heard before.

"And the sun's in the north," he said. "Is that right?"

"Well," she said. "Well, I suppose so, Mr. MacTaggart, mebbe."

"You with your scholarship," he said severely. "You should know."

"Och, scholarship! But let's see now, Mr. MacTaggart, sun in the north, yes, that could be right."

"What studies are you taking, Maggie? Are you still to be a teacher?"

"No," she said. She seemed to be nervous of him. "Physical education was what I wanted to be doing, but those dumb professors bribed me into nuclear physics. Cursèd brains, who wants them?"

"I could do with a few myself."

"You, Mr. MacTaggart! And you the wisest . . ." But the flash and the crash were almost together, drowning Maggie's words about his wisdom, and she shivered, leaning against him and away. "I'm feared of it," she said. "I always was from the time I was wee."

And he had seen her from Wee Maggie through the growing, the strange unfolding of Maggie's growing to be a tall stranger from New Zealand still afraid of thunder. ". . . I didn't hear, Maggie?"

"I was saying the cult of the body is my chief concern, Mr. MacTaggart. The body—what else is there that matters?"

"The mind," he said, "surely that matters, Maggie."

"Not to me," she said. "That's where I differ from

the ancient Greeks. But those professors in New Zealand said that unless I enlarged on the quantum theory, I couldn't keep my scholarship. Still, that only takes two or three hours a day and leaves oodles of time for callisthenics." The lightning hissed, and all the thunderbolts of heaven struck upon the Lum as Maggie clutched at him. But the thunder died, and the rain roared on, and Maggie released his arm.

"Callis . . . ?"

"Callisthenics," she said. "Free exercise for grace and muscle. It comes from two Greek words actually —Kallos, beauty; and Sthenos, strength. Well, later on I branched out a bit, but callisthenics is the real secret of my success."

"You mean your secret of . . . of reducing like?"

"Well, yes. But it's not just reducing, Mr. Mac-Taggart. We build up the right where we take off the wrong. Look at yourself now. You're the living embodiment of years and years of building the body where the body should be built."

"It could just have happened anyway," he said. He had been thinking that again yesterday before the new Maggie Oliphant arrived.

"No, it could not!" she boomed indignantly in the Lum, and the rain still roared, but the storm was passing. "I said to myself out there just now. I said: that mighty chest, those grand wet shoulders, those biceps like a wee man's thigh. He did it alone, I said to myself." She paused. "Mr. MacTaggart?"

Geordie turned to meet the stranger's sad brown eyes. "Yes, Maggie?"

"Could I just the once?" Without waiting for permission she put her finger-tips, just her finger-tips, to touch Geordie's bicep through his shirt and jacket. "Oooh!" she said, and took her fingers back.

He looked through the narrow door of the Lum, fat Maggie again beside him. "Later on you branched out a bit, you said."

"Did I? Oh, well. Oh yes, Mr. MacTaggart. I added the gentle art of self-defence. Neo-Judo, it's the latest New Zealand art or science. Nudo, we call it for short."

"Self-defence?" he said.

"Yes, Mr. MacTaggart. You see it was this way. As the callisthenics built my body beautiful, so the wee men started having ideas. A grand muckle Jock like you, Mr. MacTaggart, you wouldn't understand what wee men can be like." Then Maggie spat. She vented her feelings with a bull's-eye jet right through the rocky door of the Lum.

So Geordie was right, and Jean was wrong. She was the same Maggie Oliphant inside; and strangely enough, she said: "You were always the same to me, Mr. MacTaggart. Just as nice and kind to me when I was fat. I'm not too fat now, Mr. MacTaggart, am I?"

"No," he said. "Just right, I would say." The rain had nearly stopped.

"You were almost the only one who didn't laugh at me. That's why I never said, not even to Dad and Mum—so I could spite all the others, and they would be nice to me now I'm bonny, and so they are. Wee men! But you're just the same as you always were." Maggie sighed. "Muckle laddies," she said. "It's muckle laddies near my size I like."

"There should be plenty of young muckle laddies near your size down New Zealand way," he said.

"Aye, young ones," she said, "with the fuzz on their cheeks and no co-ordination."

"The rain's stopped," he said.   "After you, Maggie."

She did not crawl out on hands and knees, but bent herself back, far back until the law of gravity was defied, and walked out that way.   "We call it Limbo, Mr. MacTaggart," she explained respectfully.

"Is that part of Nudo?"

"Nudo? Oh yes, I mean och no, Mr. MacTaggart. It's part of who can get under the lowest bar. And I'm the girl champion. Believe it or not, I can beat the whole skinny lot of them."   Maggie chuckled.

She's still my pal, Geordie thought. He led the way back to the motor-bike, his fat pal safely behind him.

"Just five days, Maggie?" he said.

"That's all, Mr. MacTaggart. You see, this wee boy's parents they were lost at sea—well-off people with a huge sheep place, it was a tragedy. And he was too young to travel alone, so I brought him in the plane and took him to his grannie's down in Kent, and I get my flight back all for free. A nice wee boy, I just wish wee boys wouldn't turn into wee men."

"The planes make a different world of it," Geordie said.   "You in New Zealand and our Charlie in Canada."

Maggie drew in breath but did not speak.

"He's away up Athabaska way this summer."

"Is that so?"

The breeze was clean and fresh, and a rainbow curved over the sky and down to put its colours on the heather, on the very spot where treasure lay.

"It's a pity Charlie couldn't have been home. You would have had company your own age."

"Company with that . . ." But Maggie had a coughing spell. "The rainbow is bonny," she said.

They came to the bike, and Geordie spread the waterproof to make dry seats. "Hop on," he said. Then it was fat Maggie holding his waist, not the stranger from New Zealand; but he had to admit that if he turned his head, or if the world should turn its head to see them passing by, the world would see a shapely blonde on the back of Geordie's motor-bike.

He was half-way to the hill gate when a red projectile came snaking up. Geordie cursed to himself, and took prudently to the grassy verge. It was the Laird doing one of his hill climbs, extra thrills to-day on a slippery road. He skidded to a stop.

"Damn you, George. I was going to break my record." Then he noticed Maggie. "Aha," he said. "Juno Astarte riding pillion to Sir Lancelot. How come?"

"We were caught in the storm, and . . ."

"Can't hear a word you say, m'dear," the Laird bellowed. He had to know everything. So Geordie stopped the engine, and Maggie went over to tell the Laird. ". . . The thunder and lightning were just awful in the Lum."

"Well, you had a stout man to be in a tight-cornered Lum with." The Laird guffawed and shot off. Maggie blushed. She used to blush painfully at any time all over. Now she blushed bonnily in public. She was not too shy in private now, but sometimes she seemed to talk a little wildly.

"The Laird is pretty daft to-day," she said in Geordie's ear as they continued.

"Aye," Geordie said. But he was thinking about what folk might . . .

So perhaps was she. Maggie opened the gate. "Well, mebbe I'd better walk from here," she said. "Thanks, Mr. MacTaggart. Thanks for being my shield and my protector. It's new memories now I can have about the Lum. Well, cheeribye."

"Cheeribye," he said, and rode down home alone.

"Geordie! Wake up, Geordie! What's this *Nudo*?"

"Nudo's gentle art," he said, partly down the vale of sleep. "It's for to learn wee men to mind their manners."

"What's this Nudo you kept shouting?" Jean inquired at breakfast.

He had remembered enough to expect a question. "It's short for some new kind of Judo from New Zealand Maggie Oliphant was talking to the Laird about."

"Big braw lassie," Bridget said.

"Poor wee men," Jean said. She chuckled, but perhaps not just too nicely.

Geordie went to work. Ask no questions, you'll be told no lies, he thought. But why tell lies? Why tell lies when there's nothing to tell lies about? Well, because. Because, although in the eye of his mind, Maggie was fat Maggie and she always would be, she was not now fat Maggie to Jean MacTaggart. And another thing—if you have to tell a lie, tell a real good whopper, not a bad one she can check about and get still wronger ideas if the Laird has not been informed of Nudo.

I bet George Washington would have told a good one if he ever had, thought George MacTaggart. Let that be a lesson to you. But it was a lesson on the downward path.

For two days Geordie did not meet Maggie. On the third forenoon he was driving the Land-Rover to chisel a few bits of granite the Laird was wanting for a new rockery—to be keeper and stalker at Drumfechan was not just as simple as that. *Look, George, be a sport and change jobs, would you?* But it lent variety.

So he was on his way down the glen; and on her way up the glen came Maggie Oliphant. She used to puff and pant and quiver redly as she wobbled up, but now she rode her bicycle with effortless cool ease. Looking at her face to face as they stopped to exchange the time of day on the Drumfechan road, he could not deny that callisthenics had indeed brought beauty and strength to Maggie Oliphant. She wore her kilt, and a pale blue silkish blouse without sleeves to it.

"Oh, Mr. MacTaggart, I'm so glad to catch you because it has to be good-bye. Those silly bums have changed my flight, and I'm off this afternoon."

"Sorry to hear that, Maggie," he said. Yes, he was sorry. It would be the same dull glen again that the Laird complained about, and so did he inside himself. "We'll miss you," he said.

She smiled at him. "I'm not just too busy for an

hour or two," she said, "if you don't mind company, Mr. MacTaggart, wherever it is you might be going."

"Don't mind," Geordie said. "To the quarry for some granite," he explained. "You could hide your bike in the snowberry bushes."

She hid her bike off the road and got in beside him, and he turned off just ahead. I nearly missed her, he thought. Near as a whisker, I could have missed her. He put the Land-Rover in four-wheel drive, and soon they bumped up to the granite quarry. It was disused, like many of man's earlier Drumfechan works.

There was a coincidence about being here, and it was this: that on the day Henry Samson's Beginner's Course in body-building arrived in a plain brown wrapper, undersized Geordie of fourteen had come to this quarry in search of privacy to read it all through and make a start with the stretching exercises and the strengtheners. Now here he was again, thirty-two years later in the self-same place, and his companion was eighteen, young enough to be his daughter just about twice over, and yet . . . Geordie took out the hammer and the chisels and the goggles.

"Mr. MacTaggart," she said respectfully, she was always so respectful. "It's a most uncanny thing, but when I'm with you, I don't feel so much younger, I feel our ages are just telescoped together."

"H'mm," Geordie said. It was indeed a most uncanny thing the way Maggie would put into words stray thoughts of his.

"Can I help at all?"

"No, thanks," he said. "You'll have to stand away a bit in case the wee chips fly."

"Wee chips," she said. "Wee chippy-chaps."

Maggie's laugh had cheery echoes in the quarry. "Okay," she said. "I'll just have a game to myself on my lonesome, then, until you're finished."

Geordie took off his jacket, put on the goggles, and set to work while Maggie had a game to herself. He chipped along the fault, and then he got a nice clean break. The Laird wanted them in queer shapes; so that was interesting, trying to get the queerest shapes. He forgot about Maggie until a high wild cry interrupted him. It was like the joyful yelp of a dancer in the eightsome reel.

But when he turned to look, Maggie was not now yelping to some reel step. It was a dance of many dances—from stately prancing like a cavort to the controlled spreadeagle of the ballet leap, and now and then a glimpse of Scotland too—the measured precision of the Shiun Triubhas, the flurry and yelp of double ball-cuts. All over the flat bed of the quarry Maggie danced in her Black Watch kilt—like most good Perthshire men, her father had served the regiment, so Maggie was one of the precious few among common female millions of the world who had some right to the kilt she wore.

But all good things must end, and Maggie's dance ended with her back to him, arms at her sides, long legs meeting at calf and knee, the position of attention. Now she might turn about. She did, but not in the parade ground manner that Geordie had expected. Her knees dipped swiftly for the flying backward somersault, the mid-air twist, the flash of lustred limbs, the Highland yelp, and she was facing him. And then she swept a long deep curtsy. Geordie dropped hammer and chisel to applaud. "Yon was braw," he said sincerely. "I never seen the like. Now I know what you mean by callisthenics."

Maggie smiled. Her bosom—who could deny it was a noble bosom—her bonny bosom heaved. "Callisthenics can be quite hard work," she said. "I'll have a wee rest, Mr. MacTaggart."

Geordie went back to work while Maggie rested. There—that was the last block split, and she was calling him: "Mr. MacTaggart, just look what I've found!"

He turned, and what Maggie had found was an old sixteen-pound shot of his. "Did you practise here? Was this the very place you used to put the shot?"

"Yes, mostly," he said, "away from disturbance, private like."

"In this very place—just to think of it." Maggie weighed the shot in one hand, looking round the quarry and up the precipitous walls, and back at the shot, which now she tossed from one hand to the other as easily as if it were some rubber ball. "Mr. Mac-Taggart . . . Oh, Mr. MacTaggart, could you . . . ? Och, Mr. MacTaggart, would you do just one for me?"

Geordie shook his head. "It's been years and years," he said. "It must be twenty years."

"What's twenty years?" demanded the determined lassie of eighteen. "Och, Mr. MacTaggart, please—just one for me to take away down to New Zealand to remember."

"I'm not keen," Geordie said. He sought an excuse. "I doubt my shoulder's not up to it."

"That grand shoulder not up to it, Mr. Mac-Taggart, bah!" Maggie seemed vexed. She stamped her foot and her brown eyes flashed. Maggie's will was certainly her own. "That's downright mean of you, Mr. MacTaggart. Here I do a very private callisthenic dance for you, and you won't even . . ." But she stopped; she smiled again; she said in a gentle happy voice: "I know. We'll make a swop. You do one half-strength putt for me, I'll do one half-strength Nudo throw for you. That's fair enough, Mr. MacTaggart, don't you think?"

Geordie yielded without more ado. He scraped the circle with his heel, and then he took the shot from her. It felt so familiar after so many years. He made the dive and the glide and the turn, and away it went, half-strength, a beauty, and Maggie cried out in admiration, and she paced it. "Forty-five about," she said. "That's the grandest sight I ever did see. All right, fair is fair. I'll show you the Nudo. It's the most elementary throw, and it won't hurt you one little bit, you won't even feel it."

"If you fell yourself," Geordie said, "you might be getting your blue blouse dusty."

Maggie laughed. "I won't be falling, Mr. Mac-Taggart. Now all you do is give me your hand to shake."

"It doesn't seem too fair to throw a chap when he's shaking hands."

Maggie's eyes glinted again. "That just shows how innocent you are," she said. "The wee beasts start it with a tickle, shaking hands. But one wee tickle means one big surprise. I'll be as gentle as a lamb with you, though, Mr. MacTaggart, don't be nervous. Shake!"

Geordie put out his hand to shake, being careful to

keep his fingers straight, no chance of a provoking tickle, and it all happened rather more quickly than he could understand—but his elbow was grasped and she was stooping and he was rolling right over her back to be lying on the ground, no shock at all, he did not even feel it; but he felt surprised and stood again.

"That's primary Nudo," Maggie said, her arms akimbo.

"A chap would be feared to meet you some dark night," he said.

"They are," she said. "You wouldn't need to be, Mr. MacTaggart."

"I'd need to watch my Ps and Qs and tickles," Geordie said to make her laugh, and make her laugh he did, merry peals of mirth in the granite quarry.

"Mr. MacTaggart, you're a scream." But she was soon thoughtful again. "I know," she said, staring at him. How devoutly Maggie stared at him. "I've got it now. You do one full strength for me, and I'll do one full strength for you. I'll have to think a good one up: Got it! *Advanced Nudo throw to strangulation*, this one's called, but not in your case, it won't hurt you one teeny weeny little bit, I promise."

Geordie yielded against his judgment. He was old enough to know better than to put the shot full strength with muscles untrained these twenty years or more, but Maggie seemed to have him brainwashed, she was such a determined cheerful imaginative lassie, always making a yes of the no you meant.

It was a beauty, and he heard his shoulder click, no harm done, though. "Two feet farther," Maggie said. "That makes forty-seven in ordinary shoes.

I bet you could win the Olympic Games all over again to-morrow morning. I think you're just wonderful, Mr. MacTaggart." She picked up the shot and putted it away so gracefully and easily, good-bye shot. "That's that," she said, and Maggie sighed. Then she stared at him, her brown eyes sad, and yet inscrutable. She took a deep breath, and was perhaps a little nervous. "Shake!" she said again.

The Advanced Nudo Throw to Strangulation was still quicker, yet much more complicated, and Geordie rolled or cartwheeled over Maggie, and Maggie cartwheeled over him to twist, lithe as an eel, her fingers at his throat. He saw her face against blue sky. "I just squeeze there," she said, "and that is curtains." Her eyes bored into him. Was it to be strangulation? "Och, Mr. MacTaggart, I can't hold out a single second longer. I just can't help it."

There was no lethal squeeze. Her hands moved to his cheeks, and Maggie kissed him. She kissed him with soft passion, all six foot of bonny Maggie pinned him helpless, and she kissed him with soft passion.

"Yoo-hoo, George! George, Yoo-hoo! Good God!"

Maggie stood up to smooth her kilt, entirely self-possessed, she did not turn a hair, and said: "Advanced Nudo Throw to Strangulation is my name for that one, and Mr. MacTaggart is the aptest pupil."

Geordie scrambled to his feet and took one look at the Laird, who stood above the quarry. The Laird was puffing out his cheeks, and he was blotchy pale, and he was muttering, "*What's Nudo?* was the very question."

"Nudo is short for Neo-Judo, a gentle art of self-defence, the very latest thing." Maggie seemed vexed with the poor old Laird. "Does that answer the Laird's question?"

"It wasn't mine." The Laird's face was ruddier again. "MacTaggart!" he barked. "Did you find time between lessons to cut my granite?"

At the Laird's high ferocious bark, which, like Christmas, came but once a year on the average, you found yourself hopping, and Geordie hopped, glad of action, to tell the truth. He went over to the Land-Rover to drive it to the granite blocks, and something else had changed, alas. She was no longer fat Maggie when his back was turned. She was new bonny Maggie who had kissed him with soft passion. The Laird came just in time, thought Geordie. He was strangely moved by sin's embrace, and cheated too. Would the Laird have seen for sure? Why else would the Laird be angry?

"All ready, sir," he said, letting down the tail-gate. But when he bent to lift the first granite block—a mere nothing to him, perhaps a hundred and twenty pounds—his right shoulder clicked again, this time most painfully, and he struggled with the rock.

"I'll help you, Mr. MacTaggart." With Maggie's help he was able to spare that shoulder, that accursed ageing shoulder, all her fault. Now the granite was loaded, and Maggie sat behind, and Geordie drove, the Laird beside him.

"I have to go into Perth this afternoon, so I told your father I would drive you. Would about two be all right, Margaret?"

"Just fine," she said. "The Laird is very kind." If Geordie felt awkward, and he did, Maggie seemed calm and gentle and at ease. "It's just here I hid my bike," she said, and Geordie stopped. As a farewell gesture he went to fetch her bicycle from behind the snowberry bushes, but Maggie got there with him.

"Good-bye, then, Maggie," he said. "I hope you have a good flight back."

He put out his hand, and for a second Maggie's eyes took on an impish gleam that might mean Nudo; but then they changed, and Maggie's eyes were wet, and she said: "You make me say and do the queerest things. Good-bye, dearest dearest Mr. MacTaggart."

So that was good-bye to bonny Maggie, and Geordie drove in some anxiety, expecting the Laird to pounce, but the Laird held his fire for once, a dangerous sign.

"Stop here," he said near the Big House. "I suggest you kick the rocks out if you don't feel strong enough."

"I strained my shoulder," Geordie said, kicking out rocks.

"Shoulder of mutton dressed as lamb," said the Laird of Drumfechan icily.

". . . It was this way, sir . . ." There seemed nothing else to do but make a clean breast of it to the Laird, about swopping a half-strength shot for a half-strength throw, and so on. But he stopped short of the ending, which the Laird might not have seen at all, which might never have happened at all. But if those kisses were only in his imagination, Geordie was certainly a guilty party by imagination.

"H'mm," said the Laird, inspecting his handiwork. "You cut those rocks well, most interesting eccentric shapes. You are truly a man of parts, MacTaggart, and you have made a signal contribution to my new

H

rockery, my neo-rockery, or my nockery as I shall call
it." But for once the Laird did not seem to find his
own bad joke amusing. "George!" he said. "You
have been playing fast and loose with that poor girl's
affections."

"I never meant to," Geordie said. Maggie tricked
me into it, he nearly said, but a man must protect a
woman's honour.

"Any bloody fool," said the Laird, "not excluding
George MacTaggart—any BF could see that Margaret long cherished a colossal crush on you, and now
a consuming passion for you. Don't tell me you didn't
know that?"

"But it was always more like uncle-like. Well, I
mean even when the Laird arrived, it was Mr. Mac-
Taggart she was calling me."

The Laird gave one short neigh of laughter, but
continued sternly: "If you go sheltering in a Lum
with an attractive young woman who is dotty about
you, surely you must know that the Lum will reek,
that smoke will soon yield to flame, that the chimney
or the quarry will go up. Surely you know that."

"Well, I didn't, sir," he said. She got me into the
Lum too, he thought, but who took her to the quarry?
"And besides."

"Besides what, George?"

"Besides, I'm human too." Bonny Maggie kissed
him with soft passion. Stop that, now, he thought.

"Indeed, George," said the Laird, more like his
kindly self. "And I can't say I blame you, and I
know that charmin' gel was hell-bent on seduction—
albeit innocent, perhaps maybe. But they used to say
—they used to say, y'know, in my salad days, that

the bigger the gel, the heavier she tumbles, stands to reason in a way."

And that brought to Geordie's mind another one who tumbled heavily long ago, and she was Helga Sorensen, the girl shot-putter, and a bonny lassie then, a lassie so like Maggie Oliphant was now, and Jean . . . "What, sir?"

"You're broody, George. Snap out of it. I was saying that while I sympathise with you to some degree—a temptatious age the middle forties, as I well remember—I cannot be party to such shenanigans in my own bailiwick, or my wee but 'n ben, in kaleyard terms. This sort of thing must stop, George, however human you may feel."

"Right, sir," Geordie said.

"When provoked beyond endurance by those rascals, you tossed whole platoons from the Roman Brig. Stated otherwise, you start slowly, but once begun, take a bit of stopping. Therefore, between now and two o'clock avoid Miss Oliphant at all costs, lest she provoke you into a far more dangerous encounter, and she would, y'know, at the drop of a hat—the best of them are not gentlemen like us, as I keep trying to din into your quixotic head."

"The Laird won't say anything to Maggie?"

"Of course not, idiot. By the way, there might be a small spot of trub awaiting you at home. When I met Jean *en route* to my fact-finding mission at the granite quarry, she asked me to explain this Nudo cult that Margaret had been telling me about. No such thing, I pleaded ignorance, and Jean's fair face grew dark. I had never heard of Nudo till I saw it in the torrid flesh. Nor, I fancy, had that delightful gel until she thought it up for your benefit. Why didn't you warn me, George? What happened?"

"Well, sir, I got kind of flustered, not wanting mountains out of molehills."

"So you told a rebounding fib, no surer way of making mountains."

"What should I say to Jean?"

"That's easy," said the Laird. "Reduce the mountain to a molehill. Make a bluff joke of it."

"But I wouldn't want to be laughing at young Maggie. Maggie's decent."

"Yes, George. But that, I'm afraid, is exactly why you have to do so just a bit. It's a decent woman who causes a decent woman just to ponder. And had I not appeared in totally pained innocence at the granite quarry, might you not now be faced with a bluffing job beyond your inexperienced capacity?"

"That's true, sir," Geordie said. It was true, and Maggie kissed him with soft passion caught in time.

"You can use me too, George, if you like. I mean we're on the same side after all. Say I remembered later that of course Margaret mentioned Neo-Judo (we prefer that term, I think), but the dear gel mentions so much so amusingly in the course of conversation that one tends to forget odd things. Then at a suitable opportunity I shall confirm to Jean. Lastly, may I say, MacTaggart, that the road to hell is strewn with ill-told whoppers. They're not your forte, so don't tell 'em. If you tell 'em, tell 'em bluffly."

"Verra good, sir," Geordie said.

So Geordie started home at dinner-time, but the Laird called after him. He called: "Knock, Knock, George!"

It was a daft game you sometimes had to play with him. "Who's there?" Geordie said, displeased.

"Judo—Nudo," said the Laird.

"Who's Judo—Nudo?"

"Judo's Nudo in my Nockery," said the Laird of Drumfechan, and his cackles followed for some distance, and Geordie's shoulder was now very sore, but he would have to hide that ache from Jean.

Then he saw a glimpse of pale blue along the winding path, and he dived for cover in some rhododendrons. He lay there while temptation passed him, oh temptation passed him, oh temptation passed him by. "Damn that daft old spoilsport Laird!" she was muttering as she passed him by. Geordie went home to tell 'em bluffly.

BOOK TWO

★ I ★

Another year went by, and Charlie was home for three weeks. He had written once: *I think the only real people are the ones who stay at home.* Perhaps you did seem like an anchor to the wanderers. But when they came back—the young, the strong, the sure from a world you did not know and never would—and they were here a moment to liven the quiet place, and gone again for another time, who seemed to be the real ones?

So the summers and the winters passed, and Bridget started school, and Charlie was into his last year of Forestry across the road in Canada, and Jean was fine, and life at Drumfechan was the same as ever, just as grand and vexing to enjoy and to endure.

Then in December the Laird fell ill. It was some kind of virus that became an obstinate pneumonia, wasting his thin body. The Laird's stockbroker nephew from London came, wearing new suits and grave expressions, not a bad chap; and perhaps he hoped secretly, as those who will follow, hope—that the Laird would die. Geordie thought that and did not say it. But Jean said it to him in the dark of night. "Mebbe so," Geordie said to his hot-headed Jean.

The Laird mended slowly in the house where he was born, but late in March he was well enough to take

the long sea voyage that the doctor ordered. Well
enough? He could not manage even down the front
door steps, so Geordie picked up what there was of
him. "No Nudo tricks, if you please, MacTaggart,"
the old devil muttered.

"What was yon joke you and the poor Laird were
having?" Jean asked on the way back from the station.

"He said: *Just imagine I'm bonny Jean*," said
Geordie, not too bad a whopper, that one, and she
took it for gospel.

As age slinks in, so does time sneak faster, but those
months without the Laird crept by—no daft notions
to keep you guessing, no referee to rule the roost.
After the dam was finished, and after Charlie grew
up and went away, the Laird had grumbled that the
glen was dull. But it was dullest without the Laird
himself.

He sent picture postcards to everyone from his
ports of call around the world. *Feeling better—feeling
fine—in rude health—ruder health—rudest health—
positively portly* was the little he said about himself,
and little too about the places. The Laird mostly
wrote something linked to home, and often pretty
Lairdish, like the hula-hula dancers to the Rev.
MacNab—*Drumfechan Games, Hawaiian style*. The
Minister giggled about that for weeks. And to Geordie
a picture of that huge long bridge at San Francisco:
Try pushing them off this one, George. And yet they
weren't quite like the Laird's dry humour.

"The Laird is wearying for home," Jean said.
"I think he just says it about feeling fine. I wish he
would get safely back."

"Och, the Laird will," Geordie said, with a sureness

he did not feel about a man after grave illness at the age of seventy-seven—and too much rich food, Geordie's mother feared—and the fancy folk who would be on the ship, he never liked them, in Jean's opinion—and mebbe too many wee drams to be good for him, suggested Bridget, which brought the house or the cottage down, and Bridget a rebuke from her mother. They were anxious for the Laird, and perhaps for their own sake too.

But one night in May the cable came. Jean took it on the telephone. "*Who* for?" she said, and the voice repeated something, and Jean gave a snort and wrote it down. "Aye, it must be for Geordie," she said, "because I ken fine who it's from."

The cable said: MACTAGGART THE GREAT SCOTLAND HAD OCEAN FLESHPOTS AM JETTING HOME . . . and it gave the ETA at Prestwick, no signature.

"The Laird seems back to himself again," Jean said. She thought the address was funnier than Geordie did, and again it did not quite somehow seem just like the Laird.

Once upon a time there had been a chauffeur at Drumfechan, but now Geordie drove on state occasions, and this certainly was one, so he washed the old Humber limousine. "Please, Geordie, could I come?"

"H'mm," he said. The Laird would be pleased to see Jean, he knew, but . . . "You'll not get excited and do daft things'"

"Och no," she said. "Honest injun, Geordie, promise!"

"Very well, then," he said. So on the appointed day they set off across Scotland to the airport, Geordie

in his best suit and stalker's cap of Drumfechan tweed,
and Jean in a blue coat and skirt, and scarlet pretence
of a hat. At forty-eight she could still look good
enough to eat, or the like of that, and well she knew
it, which made half the reason.

The monster touched down with a spurt of smoke
from tyres, and Jean clutched Geordie's arm, but all
was well, and there was a gigantic whooshing as it
slowed to turn this way, to trundle, whining, to swing
laboriously at last, to stop, and life died out of the
ungainly beast. In next to no time the doors were
open, and passengers started coming down—old and
young, bronzed and pale and pink and dark, the brisk
and the untidy—and all had crossed the Atlantic
Ocean to straggle on foot with tired relief to a Customs
shed on one of Scotland's sunnier mornings. It must
have disgorged a hundred of them, and no more came
and still no Laird, and again doubts crossed Geordie's
mind about the Laird coming home.

"That's him!" Jean screamed.

"H'ssht, wumman," he muttered. Folk in the
crowd had looked and whispered and looked again,
it was Geordie's fate since that damned disgrace he
made of himself at the Roman Brig a few years ago,
and it would take wild horses or the Laird's return to
drag him into public nowadays; and now they were
all staring at Geordie MacTaggart with a screaming
wife. Jean had forgotten her promise to behave herself, but what could you do but growl and bear it?
Geordie growled, and the people near drew back,
perhaps because of his warlike reputation, but Jean
paid not the slightest heed.

The Laird came across the tarmac with a royal escort,

or it was an escort of two very bonny stewardesses, one carrying the Laird's hat and coat, and the other his black brief-case, and they were in fits of laughter. The Laird looked just fine, making sly quips to the opposite sex.

"Yoo-hoo," Jean called in the Laird's own call; there she went again.

The Laird stopped, looked up and broke from his escort to the wooden barrier. "Jean, my dear child! And the man himself— Hail, George! So you got my cable."

"It came right through," Jean said.

"To the Customs shed, sir, please! No communication is permitted." It was a policeman.

"Ah, pshaw, man! Who do you take me for, Fidel Castro's baby brother?" There was some laughter at this, but the Laird raised a hand for silence: "Let me introduce my two guardian angels of the aether, perfectly charmin' gels . . ."

"It's all right, Officer. He'll come quietly for us." So they each took an arm. "Be nice now, Laird," one said, and they led him in the right direction.

"The Laird seems just like his old self again," Jean said, going downstairs.

"Aye," Geordie said.

"Are ye not thankful, then?"

"Aye," Geordie said. He was thankful to see the Laird like his old self again, if not more so, but he was vexed about Jean's behaviour, but if he said anything she would just be worse. "It seems the Laird's getting the VIP treatment."

"What for would the Laird of Drumfechan not be getting the VIP treatment?" she demanded indignantly, so Geordie who could say no right, gave up.

The last passenger off was the first one through, and Jean gave a small whimper like a bairn, holding out her hand, and then she threw herself to hug the Laird and she kissed him on both cheeks, what a way for the gamekeeper's wife to behave, even leaving a smudge of lipstick on the Laird.

"Well, George," he said. "How are you, m'boy?"

"I'm fine," Geordie said. "You're looking grand yourself."

"Home," said the Laird, "almost home." And there was a happiness in the Laird's thin face, no thinner than before the illness, a sadness too that meets with happiness. "Well," he said briskly. "Let's get cracking. But first I must bid farewell to those resourceful poppets, talk about customs brokers."

Geordie went to fetch the car, and put in the Laird's bags, and the Bobby said: "Here'll do fine, Geordie. I'll mind it masel."

Then he went back for the Laird and Jean. Somehow you would have expected the Laird to look out of place among all these worldly travellers, as different from him as chalk from cheese; or be uncomfortable, the way Geordie felt himself, but not a bit of it: the Laird was very much at ease and master of the situation, a lanky old eagle in his green Black Watch tweed, saying good-bye to the two stewardesses, who agreed that if the Laird could only be aboard, every flight would be a riot; and they said polite how-d'you-do's to Geordie, and turned to the Laird again with a kind of young woman's delight in him that was nice to see.

There was an announcement on the loudspeaker "That's us for London," said the fair one.

"We must simply literally fly," the dark one said, and off they literally flew.

"I do love good women, George, don't you?" the Laird said loudly in the crowded place.

"Whiles," Geordie said, and there was a titter. It was a grand pleasure to see the Laird again, but even that was spoiled a bit for Geordie, spoiled by the Laird himself and spoiled by Jean, drawing attention to him. They never knew how much he hated being known wherever he might go, called by his first name, asked for his autograph, not allowed decent obscurity like other folk. And all why? All because once long ago he put the shot farther than anyone else in the world; and once, not so long ago, he was provoked into losing his drunken temper with a few wee men. And who provoked him? So they even made a song about it, "Geordie at the Brig." A smash hit everywhere, not only Scotland. And if you stood a head and shoulders above the crowd, how could you help being conspicuous? Geordie followed the Laird, who was nearly as tall as him; and then he held the door.

"Let's sit in the back, Jean, shall we?" said the Laird. "I think we're out of favour."

So Geordie drove off, and people waved. They waved to him, calling: "Cheerio, Geordie!" He raised his hand once, but neither smiled nor waved nor scowled, which last was what he felt like.

"Sorry, George," said the Laird from behind. "I know it's hellish for you, and you can't escape it, but damned old idiot, I keep forgetting."

"Me too," said Jean. "I forget because he's just Geordie to me."

"Wherein lies the proof of the MacTaggart pudding," said the Laird, and they all had a good laugh in the old black Humber limousine.

After that the Laird wanted to know about everything and everyone, first Bridget and Charlie, and then all the news of the glen, or all the news and gossip that it was proper for a Laird to be told, and it was an entertainment on the journey home to listen to Jean not quite telling what the Laird was on to in a flash. And then they stopped talking. "You should have a wee sleep now," Jean said, as to a bairn.

"I will," said the Laird, and he gave a sigh. "Wake me when we turn up the river."

But the Laird was awake again before that.

"How does the Laird feel in himself?" Jean asked in the formal way as they turned now to climb beside the River Fechan. It was the moment for the question, coming home.

"I still tire easily," he said. "But otherwise as good as new. Or better expressed: as good as second-hand jumble sale."

And Geordie thought about the Laird, of how in his young days he had travelled far, to soldier in India, to fight a war and come back with the wounds and medals. And then for many years the Laird had hardly left Drumfechan. While others of his age and kind and gifts had risen to be Governors and Admirals and all the rest, and even one Prime Minister—the Laird had stayed at home to run the place according to his fashion, which grew more peculiar. And there were plenty who used to mock him behind his back, calling him an idler—*spiv* was the word nowadays. But who were they? They were mostly the ones who thrust on ruthlessly to success, and some had done great things for their country or themselves or both. But the Laird had done little. Then illness took the Laird away; and it was only then, it was only now when the Laird was coming home that you could see that perhaps the Laird had done more for human truth than the ambitious ones had ever done.

The Laird said nothing and Jean said nothing and Geordie said nothing as they drove up the valley of Drumfechan, another summer bursting into growth. And here, below the gamekeeper's cottage was one small girl with a Union Jack, both in tired dejection until the gamekeeper, chauffeur, etcetera, sounded the horn. "Hi, Laird!" Bridget screamed.

"It wasn't us put her up to it," Jean said.

So the Laird of Drumfechan came home again.

Above the Piper's Pool there was a placid reach, a good place for trout. But then the river narrowed, swung hard left against the bank ahead, and plunged down a gorge into the pool. When the river was high, you could fish it from the other side below the Piper's Cottage. But at low water there were boulders to check the line, so you crossed by the footbridge to this shingle beach where Geordie and the Laird now were.

There was a fresh-run salmon in the pool, ten or twelve pounds, about average for the River Fechan. It jumped clean out once, a bonny fish, and once there was a swirl beside the fly. The Laird cast a few more times over that place, and then he fished the pool down through. "No good," he said. "I bet it's half-way to the loch by now." The Laird was a fair good caster when he set his mind to it, but he lacked the patience and the concentration to be a fisherman, his eye distracted by some bird, his mind gone wandering away.

He came back to sit in the folding-chair that Geordie had brought for him. He was a little out of puff.

"We should rest the pool a while," Geordie said, sitting on grass above the shingle, and he handed the Laird's binoculars to him.

"Gone, I tell you," said the Laird.

Geordie said nothing. He did not think that the fish had gone.

"Still no more word of Charles?"

"Not since two weeks ago, when he was flying off to some lake in Labrador. He thought he might go to London when he first gets over, so he said. But letters keep coming for him."

The Laird smiled. "Business letters, I presume."

"Well, there's two from the company in Vancouver Island he's to work for, and one from the university. But most of the rest . . ."

"What's that I see?" The Laird put his glasses on the other bank, at the shrubs below the ruined Piper's Cottage. "A redstart, I thought as much. *But most of the rest*, you were saying. Most of the rest are from the fair sex, George, I'll wager."

"It looks like it from the writing, so Jean says." Geordie did not add that they came in twos and threes and fours with postmarks like Calgary and Saskatoon and Ottawa and Salt Lake City, different writing from each place, and some of the air-mail forms had x's scored so deep you could read them through. Jean laughed—she even liked the idea of all the lassies being daft about Charlie.

"And it bothers you, eh, George?"

"Well, sir, you mind the last time he was home, just three weeks, and there was the one in Perth, and the one at the hotel, and both of them fair desperate, and off he went without a thought to the poor lassies being unhappy. Well, I was hoping he'd be past that stage by now."

"Oh, come on, George. Charles makes the ladies' knees to knock. You can hardly blame him because one and all they throw themselves at his head with knocking knees and so on. That's the male animal in this age of licence, which I deplore, of course, which I deplore. But he's done wonderfully well, the boy."

Yes, Charlie had done wonderfully well. He had led his class the whole way through. He had worked all over Canada, East and West and in the Arctic. He had learned to fly. He was not just a woman chaser. "That's true, sir," Geordie said.

"But perhaps too much success to be altogether good," the Laird said thoughtfully. "He swans through his exams. He learns to fly in no time flat. The women collapse like ninepins. What is always easy becomes one's due. That would be my only fear for Charles."

"That's just what Jean and I were saying."

"Ah, look! The busy bobbing dipper, how I do adore him." The small dark bird had perched on a wet rock over there, bobbing, bobbing, white chest bobbing. "But to revert to Charles—how long will he be here?"

"Two months about, sir," Geordie said.

"H'mm! Two months, two kilotons of energy to be expended. But how to achieve a controlled reaction? There's the rub, George, how indeed?"

"Worrk," Geordie said. "That's the only hope. Charlie's a grand worker too."

"Phenomenal. But he finishes the job, and then his mind, it tends to wander. What form of labour would you recommend?"

"I was thinking he could mebbe help the Laird to tidy through the arboretum."

"A capital idea, George. What else?"

"He could drive the Laird round in the Mini." The Laird's licence had been taken away from him—much to everyone else's relief and his own fury—for dangerous driving on the hill road, which he considered his private property but in fact was public. Or the police inspector had come to Geordie, and would Geordie please persuade the Laird to give up driving, because they weren't wanting trouble, but . . . So, as usual, Geordie had to do the dirty work and accept hell on behalf of the Perthshire Constabulary.

The Laird growled, still a sore subject. "Well, if it has to be anyone, I'll certainly take Charles. What else?"

"Odd jobs about the place," Geordie said. "It's not too easy just to think of enough that would keep him occupied."

"How right you are. For a fortnight Charles will be a paragon, and then the itch to go walk-about will come, and he will mount that damned motor-bike." The Laird glanced over at the footbridge. "Or he will borrow my Mini with a winning smile. Wine and women, they're the very devil, as you have cause to know."

"I never was arm-in-arm with two bonny stewardesses shaped like Venus," Geordie said.

"And I never had no Nudo lessons," said the Laird. "Talking of which, I hear Margaret may be coming home to take a job at that research place, Shanwell, is it, near Kinross. Now, she and Charles might be lively company for one another."

"No, sir," Geordie said. "They hate each other's guts like poison."

"Still? You mean the memory of the elephant in her case?"

"That's right," Geordie said. "And Charlie hates her because she told on him that time he took the car. He never forgave her, and he never will. They're a real pair of haters, both of them." And he remembered that some of those who hate, love strongly too, and she kissed him with soft passion. "What, sir?"

"What a bore I am, always interrupting people's reveries. I was saying: no doubt Charles is aware of the streamlined wonders wrought by callisthenics."

"I doubt it, sir. Jean mentioned Maggie's name once the last time he was home, and Charlie said: *That treacherous fat bitch!* Just venomous, and he left the house. I doubt if he would listen to a word about her, and if he did, what difference would it make? He would hate Maggie all the more."

They watched the black water of the Piper's Pool below the Piper's Cottage, a ruin these three hundred years. The poor jilted piper played a last lament and tied a boulder to his dirk belt to drown himself in the Piper's Pool. But no salmon moved yet in the Piper's Pool. Nothing moved but the tumbling water and the quiet water.

"None of our schemes," the Laird was musing. "None of our embryo plots and plans for the occupation and the delectation of your gifted son would more than skim the surface of those kilotons. I've been thinking, George—I've been remembering how that boy could run."

"Yes, sir?" Geordie said, much interested. In the eye of his mind he saw Charlie running, the tremendous stride, the thrust of thigh. "He was fourteen the last time he was in a race."

"No, George," said the Laird with glee. "That's where you're wrong. He ran a mile last year."

"Is that so?" Geordie said.

"Don't annoy me with bland disbelief. I have told you that is so, and now I will explain. My informant tells me that last year the University of New Brunswick was or were engaged in an athletics contest—a track meet was the term he used—against some other place, an annual event of great tribal importance. The first-string in the mile fell ill, and by some bludgeoning or blackmail—not excluding the hint of a pardon for other sins, I rather gather—Charles Ian MacTaggart was persuaded to run a mile for the sake of the dear old Alma Mater and all the rest of it. To sum the matter up, he nearly lapped the field, and then eased back to ensure that his time was mediocre."

"He never told us," Geordie said.

"He wouldn't," said the Laird. "Charles has long been in a minority of one against a world that wants him to run races, an activity which he regards as a proper waste of time. I can't say I blame him, philosophically speaking, and with all due respect to his gladiator sire."

"Who would the Laird's informant be?"

"Secret, George."

Charlie himself? Someone the Laird had asked to keep an eye on him? "Would the Laird be able to say what the Laird might have in mind?"

"The Laird would. My informant—my source is the fashionable word in M I 5, I think—my source revealed further that he himself, being interested in such matters, timed the first three laps before Charles settled back to an exhausted canter, puffing and panting for fatigued effect—and the projected time for a completed race would have been a few seconds over four minutes, and that without any training whatsoever."

"I always thought," Geordie said. "I always just felt it in my bones that Charlie could beat the world if he would set his mind to it. But first he took a scunner to the races. That was just natural, mebbe, seeing through them, you might say. But then there was something else. Did the Laird notice that Charlie never ran a step at Drumfechan since the time he and Tam Burrell were in trouble, and Tam was caught, but Charlie got away?"

"Yes," said the Laird. "I had noticed that. So you think my pipe-dream for Olympic year is hopeless, George?"

"I do, sir. It's a grand idea, but he wouldn't do it. *Races are daft*, would be the first thing—and how can you persuade a laddie who thinks that?"

"Dunno," said the Laird. "I think it myself."

"And the other is the place—every step he ran, he would be reminded of leaving Tam Burrell in the lurch. He was more ashamed of that than anything. He said as much to Jean."

"They would have caught them anyway."

"That's not the point, sir. If you leave your pal in the lurch, you've caught yourself, whoever catches you."

"True enough," said the Laird. "George, you are a never-failing . . ."

"And Charlie wouldn't forget it because he hates

to fail in anything. Mebbe that's the real reason he decided long ago that races were daft."

"That seems a hard judgment, George."

"I expect it is, sir. Charlie is a closed book to me."

"An enigma," said the Laird. "All the best sons and people are. He who spills his bag of beans is beanless." The Laird chuckled. "Not too bad, eh, George? Well, I do not utterly abandon hope. It's time we had another lusty champion of Drumfechan from the stable by the Roman Brig. Now let us forget such recondite matters. I shall continue to watch my birds, and you can try for that non-existent salmon, long vamoosed."

But the salmon had not vamoosed. While the Laird had been talking and spying through his glasses, Geordie had been watching the Piper's Pool, and twice he had seen a slight extra different swirl at the lie below that hidden rock. He put on a small Silver Doctor for a bright June morning. Then he let out line, false-casting a few times until he had the length just right, dropped the fly above the rock, mended his line with a rolling flick, and he was into that salmon first time off.

"Bravo, George! Oh, bravo, I knew you'd hook it." And the Laird issued volleys of instructions to which Geordie paid no heed, and after three runs, and two silvery jumps clean out of the water, and the thrill was always as new and good, in twenty minutes he had the fish ready for the gaff, and he gave the Laird the rod to hold. "I'll try to beach it," said the Laird. That took a bit longer, but avoided the use of the gaff. The older the Laird grew, the more reluctant he was about causing pain, whether cold-blooded fish felt pain or not. But Geordie got the salmon by a gill and killed it smartly, and that was that.

They crossed the footbridge above the Piper's Pool. It had been built to replace the old one two years ago, the remains of the old one after Charlie on his last visit had been in a mood for a small excitement, and showing off too perhaps, so he had ridden the motor-bike down the narrow path, turned a right angle on to the three-foot bridge, crossed, circled beyond to make the homeward journey, which he would have done safely no doubt, had the old bridge not collapsed under the heavy bike and Charlie and his love-lorn girl-friend from the hotel.

"I can't imagine why they didn't brain themselves on those rocks," the Laird said now, pausing to look down at the storming lip of the Piper's Pool.

But Charlie—whose reflexes were mercury quick like the rest of him—had jumped the lassie clear somehow, and they swam ashore, and the motor-bike was hooked out later from the depths.

In you go and tell the Laird yourself, Geordie said when Charlie had confessed his crime. Geordie happened to be near the Big House at the time, so he and his mother went to stand at the end of the long stone passage that led to the Laird's study, and they listened. Nobody ever quite believed that the mild old Laird could hand it out until they had been on the receiving end themselves. It started quietly, it was a murmur, then one clash of cymbals, it was like the finale of one of those Beethoven symphonies the Laird enjoyed— it was a music that swelled and faded and grew again to the thunderous climax, to the mighty detonation! "*Out!*"

And out Charlie came to shamble along the passage. He passed his father and his granny in a pale cold sweat without a word. *The Laird's blue-moon punch,* Geordie's mother called it, and he certainly sorted Charlie as nobody else had ever done.

Geordie thought of that, following the Laird slowly up the path, with pauses for breath. He was getting stronger, though. He had really improved in a month since he had come home from the travels that might not have been, for all the mention he made of them.

"You never know," he said, turning at the top of the bank to look at the sweep of the river below the Piper's Cottage. It was a pretty place sometimes, a sombre place sometimes. "See a *rara avis*, possibly— perhaps forget my snoopers."

"I have the binoculars," Geordie said.

"Yes, yes, George. I was thinking up dim plots and stratagems."

So they squeezed into the Mini, and Geordie drove the Laird home along the Green Avenue. Once it had been the main road up the glen, winding back and forth, almost flat, and the old milestones were still beside it. But in the last century a straighter road was cut; and grass had long since grown to make the Green Avenue.

* 3 *

The merlin and its prey were high, in a far higher range of sky than either would frequent. The falcon climbed to stoop again; the hunted bird—a thrush or a fieldfare perhaps—broke back again and climbed again. Up and up they climbed and tumbled. Geordie watched them all across the hill at a thousand feet or more until they dwindled into specks, were gone. If the merlin tired first, its prey would live, the one hope of the hunted.

He heard the shepherd's whistle and saw his collie dogs racing to collect the sheep. Then Oliphant looked them over, black-faced ewes and their stocky lambs. In a while he came this way. Geordie waited to walk down with him.

"Wha's daein', Geordie?"

"Nothin' special, Alec. Wha's daein' wi' you?"

"Nothin' special, Geordie."

"Fine day fer it."

"Aye, fine day fer it."

"How's the lambs?"

"Och, I canna grumble. How's the grouse?"

"Och, I canna grumble."

"How's the wife, Alec?"

"Fine. How's yours, Geordie?"

"Fine. She's wearyin' on oor Chairlie. He's due ony day, but no worrd yet."

"Oor Maggie's due too, and the wife's the same, fair clockin' for her muckle chick."

"The Laird was sayin' your Maggie's got a grand job, Alec."

"Aye, and the Laird was sayin' the same aboot your Chairlie. They're a credit to us, Geordie."

"They are that, Alec."

"I'm feared, though, Geordie."

"Are ye feared, though, Alec?"

"I'm feared we're not to have just too peaceable a summer. Yon Chairlie's like a red rag to a coo to Maggie."

"And vicey-verrsey, Alec, to a bull."

"Would it mebbe be the brains they got from you and me, Geordie, that makes them jealous o' ane anither?"

"Could be, Alec. I'm no' that jealous o' your brains, Alec."

"Nor me neether, Geordie, thanks. Cheerio, then, Geordie."

"Cheerio, then, Alec."

Alec Oliphant, who had never been known to crack a smile, turned off to his house, collie dogs leashed invisibly to heel. Geordie went on. So Maggie would soon be here again.

"Yoo-hoo, George! Yoo-hoo!" It was the Laird coming out of the door near his study, and big news, from the tone. "Charles is on his way, coming up from London with another fella who wants to put in lying hours or something, telephoned early, might they land in the Toll Park? *Land anywhere you like*, said. *In one piece is my first stipulation, and watch out for my cattle beasts is my second*, same thing really."

The Laird was in a state of high excitement, darting glances from watch to sky and back.

Weeks without a word, and now suddenly. It was too thoughtless or too casual, but that was Charlie. Just let him get home safely, Geordie thought. "Due now, sir?"

"Five past twelve," he said. "Two minutes to go."

Soon a blue and silver plane circled Drumfechan. The Toll Park was in view from here, so Geordie and the Laird watched through binoculars. "Down," Geordie said. He heaved a deep breath that their boy was safely home. The door opened, and Charlie got out. He took one suitcase and a duffel bag and closed the door. The plane turned to taxi back to take off at once. Jean and Bridget were running.

"Ah, whoopee," said the Laird of Drumfechan. "Happy days are here again." He went into the house. It was like the Laird not to want to see his pal until the MacTaggarts had had him to themselves.

Charlie had been away five years, with one short visit home, and you might have expected a strangeness in him after all his learning and adventures. But it was not so. He fitted back into the house as if he had left it yesterday. And the old resentful moods were gone. Now Charlie was a man, sure of himself as he had earned the right to be. Pleased with himself? To be the apple of his mother's eye; to be Charlie Boy, his small sister's hero pal; to meet his father's deference; to have his brains pricked and prodded by the Laird's own needle wits. Charlie accepted all this. What else could he do?

So every morning he worked with the Laird in the arboretum, which was a tree garden, you might call it, with trees from round the world. And since many were North American, and Charlie was a Bachelor of Science in that particular department, the Laird hung on his every word. If all those words were about trees, then trees must be an amusing subject, because the Laird's high cackle and Charlie's merry laughter would echo often from the arboretum.

Those were the mornings. After lunch, if the Laird felt strong enough (and he was eating better, Geordie's mother said, the most important sign, she said) Charlie would take him for racing hill climbs in the Mini, or to watch birds, or to fish when the river was in ploy. The Laird asked Geordie, with much puffing out of cheeks, whether Charles would accept payment for his many labours. Geordie thought not, but would inquire; and Charlie said that he would certainly stick the Laird up for top wages if the Laird would stick him up for top entertainment. When Geordie passed that on, the Laird was as pleased as if the Queen of Scotland herself had patted him on his bony back.

Then Charlie would play or walk with Bridget until it was her bedtime, and after that he would tell them stories of the places he had been—cruising the forests of the East and West—a summer as a deckhand on the great lonely Mackenzie River—a trip he wangled to Ellesmere Island in the farthest Arctic—a fateful river called the South Nahanni, and an old prospector, crazed for the gold that he knew lay somewhere there in nuggets for the taking. Charlie could carry you off with him to those places and those people, make the deep hoot of the forest owl, the cougar's scream, the prospector's German-English. He talked a bit about the cities too, but only of Montreal with some affection. *They're new and ugly, most of them*, he said, and smiled. *Good for beating it up, is all the use I have for cities, anyway.   And you're glad you stuck to the forestry?* Geordie asked. *Yes*, he said. *Yes, I guess so, Dad, as a solid base*, his look a little clouded. About girls he said not a word at all.   *And the Labrador trip—how many of you were there?   Just the two of us, Dad.* But whether the other chap was another chap or a lassie chap was not disclosed.

It was not a fortnight as the Laird had guessed, but about ten days after his arrival that the familiar signs began. Charlie turned on the telly and turned it off; he picked up a book and put it down; he gave a gusty sigh; he went for a stroll, kicking stones idly before him on the path.

"It isn't natural for him to be home every night," Jean said. "You offered him the motor-bike?"

"Aye," Geordie said. "But I'll say it again."

This time Charlie thought he would go and have a pint at the Drumfechan Arms. No sooner had he ridden off than there was a telephone call for him. "He's just gone into Drumfechan village. Is there any message . . . ?"

"She wouldn't give her name, but she sounded like that girl the last time, the one who stayed at the hotel."

"Oh," Geordie said. Here we go again, he thought.

"He can't help it if the lassies chase him, Geordie."

"Does he turn his backside on them?"

Jean smiled a moment, but she said, "We're going to lose him soon enough. And he's started fine. I just hope he has a good last summer."

"The Laird says it's energy. He says Charlie has enough for the whole glen put together, and if we don't see that some's used up, then it'll be the same old story, sure as onions. Did I tell you the Laird's idea about Charlie running?"

"No," Jean said. "That's one of the million things you never told me."

So Geordie told her.

"The idea's grand," Jean said. "There's just one trouble—he'll never do it. And for those two reasons, like you say. Unless mebbe . . . How good is he, Geordie?"

Geordie shrugged. "All we know is a story second-hand. The Laird wasn't saying who it was that told him."

"It'll be some high heid-yin out in Canada. I bet the Laird's had somebody keeping an eye on Charlie all these years, and he never let on to us. I've thought whiles that the Laird's known more about Charlie's doings than we knew ourselves."

"That's right," Geordie said.

"But how good is he, Geordie? Would he be as good as you were at the shot-putt?"

"He might be that," Geordie said. "He might be better. But all the other chaps will have been training for years and years, and Charlie hasn't run at all."

"That could be good, though, couldn't it—him saving his strength while they used up theirs?"

"It could be or it couldn't," Geordie said. "I dinna ken. There's just one chap who might have experience

K

of a thing like yon—and that's the Minister. He coached the Glasgow team, but it was long ago."

"He coached you long ago," Jean said.

"Aye," Geordie said. "He was a grand coach too. I could ask the Minister, even if it is a waste of time."

"Once my own man beat the world," Jean said.

"It was you made me do it," Geordie said. And again now Jean's voice came to him as he stood at the circle there in Boston. "*Come away, my wee Geordie*, I heard you say it."

Jean smiled, her thoughts far away and long ago. "Once my man," she said again. "And once my boy —och, it's a daft woman's conceit, and Charlie would never run a yard for us, far less a mile."

"Fifteen hundred metres," Geordie said. "It's a hundred and thirty-five yards less, about. That's what they run in the Olympics, not a mile."

"You and your details. *It's not a mile.* It's not half past ten the now—it's twenty-eight minutes and thirty seconds to the hour of eleven. So what's the difference?"

"Ninety seconds," Geordie said. "Now bed, you wee bezzom."

"Geordie!"

"Well, what is it?" He was sliding into sleep.

"Ye ken all those letters in his room?"

"Aye."

"He hasn't opened them, not one. It seems kind of queer to me."

"Mebbe it would be like your hats," he said. "How long do they stay new?"

Jean giggled, and they went to sleep.

There was a telephone summons in the morning. "You will find me at my nockery, George." He always called it that since a certain day when Geordie had split rocks in the old granite quarry. It was now full of rare plants from the Himalayas and those places, which the Laird was given by another Geordie, a famous gardener, to try them out and compare results between Perthshire and Angus. "Damned weeds," the Laird grumbled, as gardeners tend to grumble, and he left his rockery.

"It occurred to me yesterday, George, that a certain restlessness was beginning to reveal itself, that itch to walk about we were discussing."

"Jean and I were saying just the same, sir."

"Jean and you say many things together, George. I even find my own ears burn occasionally in the watches of the night."

"Is tha' a faact, sirr?" Geordie said.

"Tha' is. Conceit, no doubt. Now listen, George. . . ."

". . . Right, sir. I was thinking—the Minister had a big experience in his time. Would I ask him to come along for his opinion?"

"A capital notion, George. So the moment you are in readiness, you make the whaup's sad cry. Do it for me now, George, just for fun."

So Geordie made the whaup's sad cry, the wild cry of the curlew.

"Perfection, George. Were I a lady whaup, you would turn my very bones to water. Until afternoon, then, George. *Auf wiederhören*, Whaup!"

The Minister was much pleased to be asked for his

opinion. "It's like old times," he said. "Do you mind the first time we put the weight together?"

"Aye," Geordie said. "And you beat me by yards and yards."

They stowed their bicycles out of sight, and walked along the Green Avenue towards the Piper's Pool. "It is two questions that we face," said Mr. MacNab, "and both are ticklish. The first—with due deference, Geordie—is the nature of the MacTaggart breed. In other words, no blasphemy or offence intended—if I say to a MacTaggart *Go*, against his will, MacTaggart often cometh, and Charlie is no exception. Mebbe the Laird can get him to run once. But to get him to train for something he looks down upon—impossible.

"Our second conundrum is not a question of will but of capacity. From his childhood we've known that Charlie is a rarely-gifted runner. But he has not run. Has he lost in physique and stamina thereby? Has he just possibly gained thereby? The case may be almost unique, I fancy, without precedent." The Minister shook his head. "Ticklish," he said.

"There's the milestone," Geordie said, "and the four-furlong mark is at the Big House. So it's a mile there and back, give or take fifty yards."

"Fine," said the Minister. "I've my stop-watch ready."

They took cover in the bushes. The Piper's Pool was just below, but not in sight. A conversation floated up.

"You mean you own the thing outright?"

"Yes, sir. I have quite a good rental deal with the flying club while I'm away."

"But surely they cost the earth?"

"It was just over twelve thousand dollars, second-hand. The dual undercarriage—floats and wheels—costs about as much as the rest of the plane."

"*Twelve thousand dollars.* Good God, m'boy, have you been robbing banks?"

Geordie was all ready to make the cry of the whaup, but he could not; for the life of him he could not.

"No, sir. Well, actually . . ."

"Mum's the word, Charles. Mum's the word. Well, actually what?"

"I sold some stories. I started writing them in camp at night, and . . ." The voice dropped off.

"How fascinating, but what kind? Adventure? Meaty stuff?"

"The former with a slight hint of the latter, sir. I stopped, though, as soon as I got the cash."

"Remarkable, Charles, remarkable."

"Actually, the plane's going to be extremely useful in my job."

"No doubt. And just possibly to seek fresh heroine material wherewith to buy bigger and meatier aeroplanes, eh, Charles?"

"Just possibly, sir. You won't mention this to Dad or Mum, though, will you?"

"My lips are sealed, old boy."

"I wouldn't mind Mum knowing, I might possibly tell her. But Dad would take a dim view, I think. He would feel that the right place for such ill-gotten gains is in the bank, not in aeroplanes. Dad's a bit strait-laced, if you know what I mean, until he gets his blood up."

"Indubitably, Charles. And I would fain that your own laces were a little more akin to Dad's. But if I were you, young fella, I would not tell Mum if you don't want Dad to know. They have been sharing secrets since the age of five, a fairly old-established firm. And any tidings about their interesting son and heir are top-secret high-priority intelligence to be communicated after lights-out."

Charlie's laugh was wonderfully hearty, and the Minister giggled in the bushes. "Old Beelzebub," he muttered.

There was silence at the river. Now Geordie made the sad cry of the whaup.

"That bird, Charles! Oh, Holy Moses, my glasses, quick!"

"Your glasses, sir?"

"My snoopers, dammit. On the Scots pine, can't you see? I believe it is, I'm almost sure it is—a crested tit, the first sighting this side of Rothiemurchus. Oh, hell's bells and utter woe!"

"What, sir?"

"I left my snoopers on the table in the hall. A crested titmouse, I'm sure it is, the most important sighting of my life . . ."

"In the hall, you said? I'll run and get them!"

"Oh, could you, dear boy? Then run! Fly like the very bats of hell! Chance of a lifetime, chance of a lifetime . . . !"

A light pounding on the wooden bridge, and here Charlie came, and a click from the stop-watch as he passed the milestone, and it was just five past on Geordie's second hand. Charlie wore his khaki shirt, his MacTaggart kilt, his green hose, light rubber-soled shoes from Canada. *Hush-Puppies*, he called them.

"A remarkable action," said the Minister. "Look

at that stride. Look at the length of that backward thrust, see the sole of the shoe almost horizontal, see the straightness of the driving leg, see the economy of body and arms. Pump, pump, pump, and away he floats. In all my born days I never saw a stronger action, Geordie. Not Bannister, not Landy—not even Snell could stride Mother Earth more impressively."

"Aye, Charlie can run."

"But can he last, that's the nub of the matter? What's his oxygen absorption, Geordie, there's the key?"

"He's kept up his piping. Wherever he went he took his pipes."

"Yoo-hoo! Yoo-hoo! Are you still there, George?"

Geordie coughed to acknowledge his presence.

"The whaup is with us. What about the Church of Scotland?"

"Here too," the Minister said.

"And a very respectable influence, if somewhat ticklish. Knock-knock, Holy One."

Geordie nudged the Minister. "Humour him, or he'll be worse."

"Who's there?" said the Minister.

"MacNab."

"Who's MacNab?"

"Mac nabbed the keys from poor old Peter." The Laird cackled with self-satisfaction beyond the Piper's Cottage. "Only one small absent friend. Oh, Crested Titmouse, where art thou? Damned Tittie took off for Rothiemurchus."

"Yon saintly old devil," said the Minister. "Yon devilish old saint! He weaves his web about us all. Ah, here is Charlie!"

Charlie had the strap of the Laird's binoculars wrapped round his wrist. He was still two hundred yards away, the legs as regular as pendulums. Charlie came flying, floating, flying.

"I say, George! As a matter of interest, had you just arrived when you made the sad cry of the whaup?"

"H'sssht!"

The Laird tut-tutted, and was silent.

"Look at that chest!" the Minister whispered. "Look at those legs! A running machine, that's what he is." The stop-watch clicked, and Charlie shot downhill to the river.

"Four twenty-six and one-fifth."

"Four twenty-five, just roughly by my second hand."

"In those clothes, Geordie—a steep bank to climb first—without a day's training—there's no doubt, no possible doubt but that he's in the Olympic class."

"He *would* be," Geordie said, "if his heart was in it."

"Ah, Charles, back so soon! How the devil did you do it? Bless you, my boy, for your thoughtfulness. But alas, that wretched bird flew away not half a minute ago. I do apologise. I was sure of it too, the one ornithological triumph of a lifetime—a crested titmouse at Drumfechan, dammit."

"But if you're so sure, sir, you could claim a firm identification."

"No, Charles old chap, that isn't on. One might make firm claims in lesser matters on what I might call presumptive evidence. But not about birds. A cast-iron certainty, or I make no claim. That's my rule, and always will be. Not a bad precept to take through life, young fella."

"No, sir," Charlie said. "I mean, yes, sir."

"Well, that's that, another disappointment. Now I suppose I should flog the pool again while you get your breath back. You must be tired after that phenomenal performance, fruitless through no fault of yours."

"I'm not tired, sir. I'll fish it, if you'd rather."

"I would much rather. At my time of life I prefer to sit upon the sidelines, lending encouragement and bad advice while the river bumbles by. So on you go. Y'know, Charles, I was thinking just then. I had a thought as you came flying down the hill—a foolish thought, no doubt."

"What was that, sir?"

"Well, for my sins I'm Chieftain of the Games again this year. For my sins, indeed, because thanks to the bungling mismanagement of others, the gate has been steadily falling off. A shot in the arm is what we need, some new dynamic appeal to the imagination. As you came, fleet as Mercury down that path, a notion occurred to me—*They* have an Olympic Torch. Why shouldn't we have a Drumfechan Torch? Why not pay this graceful tribute to your birthplace, streak along the Green Avenue, and across the Roman Brig and circle our arena amid the plaudits of the hoi-polloi, and present our flaming torch to our flaming Chieftain, myself, of course. What the devil are you laughing at? I mean this, Charles. I am in deadly earnest."

"It wouldn't be a race, sir, would it?"

"A *race*? Good God, no, I despise such competitive stupidities, although as Chieftain I must condone them. But no, a ridiculous idea, I take it back. These games are a hellish headache, but why should you be victimised . . . ?"

Geordie and the Minister walked back to their bicycles. "The Laird of Drumfechan now seems to be restored to full health, for which we may be thankful."

"We may be thankful for the restoration of the health. What with him and Charlie, it looks we're in for a busy summer. Well, cheerio, Minister."

"Cheerio, Geordie. First stop Jean?"

"That's right," Geordie said. He rode home to tell his true and faithful wife about aeroplanes and stories and the Chieftain's flaming torch.

* 4 *

The next morning Geordie was out by seven-thirty. He walked down the glen to the old granite quarry, then climbed south-east through birches and bracken and over the wall, and he was on to the open hill. He walked all morning, clear to the march with Altnadean; then back by the hill loch where he saw and stalked and shot a great black-backed gull, a bad customer and a wary one.

He crossed the hill road and climbed again to swing north. He was near the ridge they called the West Tully, where he had caught poachers once, when he saw another poacher. He came over a crest, slowly as always, and there, waddling about the heather was a golden eagle. It was not having a constitutional, the killer eagle was on killing bent, and it quartered the deep heather carefully and systematically, the merciless head cocked, the cold eye intent, until it pounced, tossed the grouse high, and hopped with spread wings to feed. Geordie could have frightened off the eagle, but why bother? If it was not that terror-stricken grouse, it would be another. The Laird would be pleased to hear about the black-backed gull—*rapacious scavengers*, he called them. And Geordie would be pleased to tell the pained Laird about his beloved golden eagle hunting on the ground.

There had been a good hatch, and there would be a fair number of grouse, eagles notwithstanding, but nothing to the old days. *Go-Baack*, they called about the hill, and the calls fell behind him. He had walked ten miles, and was ready for his dinner.

"Charlie's away," Jean said. "He took the notion after his breakfast—just for a couple of days, he said." She spoke in the casual way that meant she expected Geordie not to be too pleased.

"Did he take the bike?"

"No. He said he would thumb a ride to Edinburgh if he could. And I'm thinking he could—yon lassie went by in a black MG soon after he walked down the road."

"It's not right," Geordie said.

"No, it's not right. But the world's different nowadays. They all do it, Geordie."

"Some of them do it," Geordie said. "And Charlie's one, and that doesn't make it right. Besides, what about the poor lassie when he's had his fun and dumps her for the second time? I don't like it, Jean."

"Nor me neither. But there's nothing we can do about it—nothing, Geordie."

"*Itchy foot to walk about.* Itchy foot to kick about the seat of the pants is what these young chaps are needing."

"Come away then, auld chap, and eat yer dinner."

After dinner Geordie cleaned his gun. "Maggie Oliphant's home," she called from the scullery. "Did you see her, Geordie?"

"No," he said. "Did you?"

"Aye. I was talking to your mum, and Maggie came in."

There was a small shiver in Geordie's neck, for no reason at all, but there was a shiver. "How does she seem?" he said.

"Och, fine. She kept us in stitches about the voyage from New Zealand. A natural comic, Maggie is. And you can't just tell when she's having you on."

"H'mm," Geordie said. Maggie's nature was earnest underneath, unless Maggie had changed. He put his gun together and stood it in the rack. ". . . What, Jean?"

"I was saying I wish they weren't at daggers drawn. They get on just grand with the rest of the world. Why not with one another?"

"It's too old a story," Geordie said. "But mebbe they will."

"No, they won't. When I said, *Charlie's home*, you should have seen the look go over her face, and she said hoity-toity, just full of hate: *By aeroplane now, I understand*. What's wrong with him coming in an aeroplane?"

"Would she mean it was stuck-up?"

"*Stuck-up.* Charlie's no more stuck-up than you are." Jean came into the kitchen. "*Than you are*," she said again. "I wonder if that could be behind it."

"How do you mean?"

"Och, nothing," she said. "Just Sugar-Daddy's fatal charm. What's on this afternoon?"

"I've logs to split," Geordie said. "That's one thing about the Laird—he needs a fire more now."

"Aye," she said. "That's often a sign."

He went to the walled courtyard behind the Big House, where the woodshed was and a pile of logs outside it. They were beech, easy to split. He halved them with one stroke, and quartered them with another. It was a hot afternoon in the sheltered place. Geordie had a mind to take his shirt off, and then he thought he wouldn't. There was not much interest in the job, and yet a small satisfaction to the wielding of the axe. Soon he had enough to last the Laird a month.

"Hallo, Mr. MacTaggart." Well, there she was. Here was Maggie Oliphant herself, standing at the entrance to the courtyard.

"Maggie!" He set the axe into the chopping block. "Splitting a puckle logs," he explained.

"I was watching you," she said. "You're a pure artist, Mr. MacTaggart, with the axe. I'm glad it's not my head across that block to be chopped clean off like cottage cheese, and my life's blood rushing-gushing out in jets."

He could not but look at Maggie's slender neck. "Yon's a queer notion to be expressing," he said. It was indeed.

Now Maggie's lifeblood rushed if not gushed in a most becoming tide up past that neck to her bonny face. "I say daft things I don't mean at all." She came to shake hands with him, and then she held on to his hand, and stood on tiptoe to give him a kiss. "Mr. MacTaggart, you make me so goddam shy," she said, another surprising comment. It was a nice soft kiss, and Maggie had a nice soft scent about her. She stood away from him to study him while Geordie glanced to see with some relief that no one was in sight beyond the archway. "You haven't changed," she said. "You never will."

"You're looking fine yourself," he said, and so she was in a thin dress with bonny patterns all curving faithful to the bonny shape of Maggie, and Maggie stared at him with soulful eyes. It was three years since she had last been home, time enough for a lassie to learn some sense. But now, straightaway, she was stalking him again. It had to be stopped this afternoon, this very afternoon, for good and all. "You're mebbe a wee thing scrawnier than last time," Geordie said judiciously, to make a start.

"*Me scrawnier?*"

"It'll be all those exercises. Too much is too much of anything. Too much fat becomes too much lean through too much physical jerks."

"But, Mr. MacTaggart!"

"I've the kindling still to split," he said. "Make yourself at home, Maggie, take a pew. You can sit on my jacket if you like."

"Oh, could I?"

A small mistake, she seemed to have reverence even for his jacket. Geordie sat himself on a log before the chopping block, held his axe near the head and began to slice off kindling, each sliver toppling before the last had fallen. "Split, split, split," she said, "just as neat and regular as a machine."

"It's one of the things I'm good at," Geordie said complacently. "Well, Maggie, what's your news?"

"My best news is to be home again," she said.

"Och well, you'll soon get over that. The novelty wears off."

The pile of kindling grew apace. Maggie sat on his jacket on the pile of logs. "They make a rather knobbly resting-place for my anatomy," she said, and re-arranged her limbs, and Geordie kept on splitting sticks.

"The Laird seems well again," she said.

"Aye," he said shortly. "The Laird is well enough. Should be after yon long voyage."

"And how's wee Bridget?"

"Spoilt," he said. "She gets her own way a sight too much."

"And you, Mr. MacTaggart. In yourself, I mean, how are you?"

"I haven't changed," he said. "You just told me so."

Maggie sighed. Keep to it now, he told himself. "That should do them a week or two," he said. "And a fat lot of thanks I'll get." He filled the kindling box and stowed the axe and dusted off his hands. "Well, Maggie," he said. "I hear you've got yourself a fancy job. Making atom bombs, it'll be, I suppose."

"No, Mr. MacTaggart, it will not." Maggie sounded hurt, but he did not look at her.

"What then? Bigger and better H-bombs, is it?"

"My field is peaceful. My field's just as peaceful a search for heat and power in a very difficult, complicated way as you splitting logs for firewood is a peaceful means to heat and power in a very simple way."

"Well, thanks," he said. "Would it be possible to explain your field so a simple chap could understand?"

"Mr. MacTaggart, that wasn't what I meant. Oh well, never mind. The research work I'm doing now is on the harnessing of the Thermo-Nuclear Reaction, which in simple terms means being able to use all the vast heat of the H-bomb slowly. Oh, we're a long way from it yet. But it will come, and when it comes we shall have a limitless source of power. The possibilities are just infinite, Mr. MacTaggart—that is, in ordinary terms."

"What about the miners?" he demanded.

"What about the miners, Mr. MacTaggart?"

"Out of a job," he said. "And not just miners, every working man like me—I was reading where it spoke about the injustices of automation—fifty million human souls in this island condemned to idleness by a handful of scientists like Maggie Oliphant."

"I don't think that's very fair of you, Mr. Mac-Taggart. I just do the job I'm qualified to do, like everybody else."

"And you're paid for it, and so am I, and the next job I'm qualified to do is pick up the eggs. Would you care to stroll along with me, Maggie?"

Maggie stood and handed him his coat. Her eyes were not soulful now, nor did they flash fire as he had seen them do. Maggie's eyes were hurt and puzzled. "Well, I suppose so," she said, and shrugged her wide braw bonny shoulders.

Now remember, Geordie thought. She's only like a painting or a statue to admire, that's all. And he led the way, and she followed, silent as a bonny ghost behind him, until: "Mr. MacTaggart!"

"Ugggh?"

"I don't think you can be feeling just yourself to-day."

"Not myself to-day?" Geordie turned, stepping back to avoid collision. "Let me tell you I am feeling *just* myself to-day. I'm nearly fifty years of age, and

I feel them, every one. You look at that!" He held his hand out straight. The fingers trembled. Geordie's hand shook like a drunkard's in the ghastly morning. "Do ye ken the cause of that?"

"No," she said with kindly pity. "No, I don't."

"Nuclear fall-out," Geordie said. "Your own poison, Maggie, not that I'm accusing you."

"But, Mr. MacTaggart, that's absurd, just lunacy. There could be no possible connection, even if the levels were to rise a thousand . . ."

"Am I not entitled to my own opinion?"

"Yes. Oh yes, Mr. MacTaggart. Yes, of course." Once again Maggie followed, wary ghost to the palsied crackpot. Geordie collected the eggs, took a near-kick at a hen, and led the way once more across the field, and through woodland paths.

"Are you keeping up your callisthenics?"

"My callisthenics? Good heavens, no. Why, Mr. MacTaggart?"

"Well, the last time you were home you said the cult of the body was your chief concern. You said: *The body, what else is there that matters?* You said you had no time for the mind, that was where you differed from the ancient Greeks. And what about the gentle art of self-defence? What about the Nudo?"

"*Nudo*, Mr. MacTaggart, I just don't understand. But wait now. . . . Oh, my God!"

"Margaret," he said, turning on her once again, and he was dismayed to see that poor Maggie had gone pale. "That is twice this afternoon that you have used the Lord's name in vain. I will have no more blasphemy, if you please."

Maggie stared at him as usual, but not as usual,

and her colour was coming back, and she was a very bonny, very angry lassie. "It's all your fault," she said. "You made me nervous and I lost my head and told daft stories. It's all your blame."

"Is it my blame if a silly lassie tells daft stories? No, it's not my blame. It's just very boring, as the Laird would say."

"Well, let me tell you, Mr. George MacTaggart, that there are plenty of intelligent men who don't find me very boring, or a silly lassie either."

"Well, that's good," Geordie said. They passed the monkey-puzzle tree in silence.

But Maggie tried once more. "Mr. MacTaggart, I just don't understand."

"What don't you understand?"

"Och, nothing," she said.

"Cheerio then, Maggie," he said, nodding dismissal at the back door, and he took the day's eggs into the Big House.

The next thing Geordie did on that troubled afternoon was to clean out the kennels, a messy job. The last kennel belonged to old Bess, grey-muzzled now, and a faithful friend. She went for a snuffle round about the bushes and came back and sat with dignity to watch him clean her living quarters. "You know, Bess," he said, "if good women were as little trouble as good bitches, it would be a grand life for a man." Bess wagged her tail. "Duller, mebbe," Geordie added.

"Yoo-hoo, Yoo-hoo! Where is the fella?"

"Here, sir," Geordie said.

"George, are you all right?"

"I'm fine, sir."

"George, do me a favour, would you? Stretch out an arm at shoulder level."

Geordie did so.

"H'mm.   I happened to be pottering about my nockery when young Margaret appeared, or she was passing, so I hailed the child. Well, it takes quite a lot to make that gel speechless, but she virtually was, or it came out by fits and starts and tearful outrage. She said that in the course of one horrid hour you had utterly shattered her lifelong devotion to you. She said that you were all the things that you had never been—conceited, jealous and unkind, sarcastic and fanatical, critical of your darling daughter, callous about my health, cruel to your hens. And finally, quite crackers, making wildly impossible statements about nuclear power, even automation. I soothed her down as best I could. I think I have an inkling, George, but do explain."

"Well, sir, I just wondered what Maggie would be like, whether she'd got over that old daftness, well you know. And from the first moment I could see that Maggie was wanting to start where she last left off and go on from there, if the Laird understands. And Jean had made a wee remark at dinner-time. So I just decided to put a stop to that for good and all. I hope I didn't overdo it."

"No, I fancy not, if you keep the good work up a bit. Hell hath no stinker like the name MacTaggart at the moment. It had bothered me a little, yes, I must confess it. These infatuations can be lethal, George, y'know. And a marvellous dish of young womanhood like that, where could a chap ultimately draw the line?"

"A chap mightn't want to," Geordie said. "Yon could be the reason that I did."

"And a good honest reason too, my boy. Congratulations, George. Margaret will see through it all, of course, when she simmers down from incandescence. But she will remain convinced that you were ridiculing her; and no woman's heart stays palpitating tender under that. Then she will rationalise her self-esteem by attributing your strange conduct to the difficult changes some men experience at your time of life—of which I dropped a hint."

"The Laird was more than kind."

"Not at all, old boy, always glad to help. Well, that's that, thank goodness, a small cloud off my mind. Next question: When will Charles be back?"

"I don't know," Geordie said. "I thought mebbe Charlie would have told the Laird." Like about aeroplanes and writing stories, and this and that, he did not add.

"Not a word," said the Laird. "No MacTaggart tells me anything. But we must get that boy started with his running soon. Yes, we must."

* 5 *

"So we have cleared the first hurdle with flying colours—a dubious metaphor, but it will serve. Now to the real question—is Charles potentially good enough?"

"We can't be certain," said Mr. MacNab. "Not with one single trial and the distance only approximate—but yes. It's a rare talent, Charlie's. Och yes, I'd stake my reputation on it."

"And an unblemished reputation too. What is your opinion, George?"

"I agree with the Minister. Charlie's good enough. He could have been good enough to beat the world if he had started training five years back, or mebbe just possibly if he would train hard now. But he wouldn't train properly, he wouldn't even train at all. And another thing—I'm not sure it's the mile or the fifteen hundred metres he'd be best at—it might be the five thousand or the ten. But anyway, he wouldn't do it."

"That's as may be. Now let's forget *would*. Let's think of *could*. But to settle the matter of distances. These other long shambles are pretty dim. But the mile and the fifteen hundred metres—they're what the whole world watches with bated breath. We had an Olympic champion once. By God, we'll have a champion again. So Up the Glen is what I say. Up the Glen! Let's have a noggin on it."

The Laird poured whisky. "Up the Glen!" They clicked glasses with solemnity. "Reminds me of another time the three of us held conclave, and great things came from that, eh, George, just look behind you."

The Laird referred to the photograph above the door of Geordie enraged between two policemen. But when Geordie threatened to give notice unless that picture was taken down, the Laird pleaded an old man's pride in it, and there the picture somehow stayed to remind Geordie of a shameful episode.

"Now, let us consider what we have to work with. You say that Charles has not trained. But listen! He has a pair of piper's lungs, and they are trained. The rest of his physique speaks for itself—who dare say that many thousand bush-whacking miles through the ice and snow and squelching muskeg of our Lady of the Snows have not trained that body. And vices he has none, except the healthiest. He does not smoke. He hardly touches spirituous liquors—the poor fella finds they make him sleepy and depressed. In short, like his daddy he is fighting fit in every general direction. All we need to do in my not-so-humble opinion is to polish and guide those fantastic gifts and energies to the starting post.

"That is what we have to do. How to do it is the very devil, dealing as we are with a wilful racehorse that has no time for racing. But I say racing is a habit. I say racing is like a woman or Scotch whisky, you can get to like it, even far too much. So we cross our bridges one by one. We are over the first. Charles has run once; he will run again.

"So to-morrow afternoon at, say, the quiet hour of

four, let us rally above the Piper's Pool for a first undress rehearsal."

"But the games are not for five weeks yet."

"I know, I know. But we'll get him rehearsing, first at modest speed, and then faster, again and again, day in, day out until it has become a habit. Until suddenly Charles finds that he is racing, not for tawdry personal distinction, but for the honour of the glen.

"After which bridge," said the Laird of Drum-fechan, "your next guess is as good as mine. I do know one thing—that splendid boy may not like to win; he certainly does not like to lose. So we must proceed with stealth. Our motto: *By hook or by crook to the winning post.* Agreed?"

The Minister coughed. "The cause is good. The Laird's reasoning is persuasive. But for a so-called man of the cloth our motto might be described as ticklish to endorse."

"Pay it lip service anyway, old boy. That shouldn't be too ticklish. Now, George, how is Charles after walkabout?"

"He seemed quiet at dinner-time," Geordie said. "I think mebbe Jean might have had a wee word with him, about, well, about . . ."

The Minister nodded, tut-tutting faintly.

"*Tut-tutt*," the Laird copied him, annoyed.

"And a much-needed word of Jean's, I'm thinking," Geordie said.

"Don't be such a prig, George. Charles gives the little things a treat. Would they be happier with no treats? Tell me that."

But Geordie and the Minister did not tell him that, an effective way of getting the better of the Laird, who had strict views too, except about Charlie, who could do no wrong. "No need to preen yourself just because you've turned your back on Nudo."

"*Nudo?*" said the Minister.

"Neo-Judo, old boy, a gentle art of self-defence. Otherwise entitled: *Puzzle find Sir Clifford's keeper.* But there is just one thing about our rendezvous to-morrow! I do trust—fond as I am of the dear gel —that Margaret will not appear on the scene. One glimpse of his *bête-noire*, and the already delicate matter of handling Charles would become an impossibility. I thought they might chum up at last, but each severally has expressed to me a pious—not quite the word, but the clergy is present—an impious hope that such a meeting will never occur."

"Maggie's father was saying she's gone down to Shanwell for a day or two to see the Director of that research place," said the Minister.

"Lucky fella," said the Laird. "Well, perhaps Charles could spare me half an hour this evening. I shall lead up gradually to important matters, perhaps draw him out first about his vast adopted land, concerning which he has a cynical idealism that I find refreshing."

It rained that night, and the next day the air was fresh and clean, every far hill standing out. At four o'clock the Laird, the Minister and both MacTaggarts stood at the milestone on the Green Avenue and the Laird was issuing instructions.

"Now, Charles," he said, "I would like to say, first, how very much those of us assembled here appreciate the public spiritedness that has led you to agree to be our torch-bearer, to be our brand-new ticket-selling gimmick at the one hundred and twentieth renewal of the Drumfechan Games."

"I didn't say I'd do it," Charlie said. "I said I'd run a trial for fun."

"Capital, my boy, capital. And may I say that any trial you run for fun is going to be fun for everyone. See! I wax poetical in my enthusiasm. Well, anyway, all we're after to-day is a preliminary canter down the course—from here to Drumfechan Square—thence across the Roman Brig of hallowed memory, Julius C. and George MacT., they both fought there—and into our arena.

"Now, Charles, we shall follow in the Mini, hoping to nip ahead of you at the Square. After you have made the triumphal circuit, you may expect to find your Chieftain waiting to receive the sacred torch, which you will hand over with due pomp and circumstance. How's that?"

"That's fine, sir," Charlie said. "No sacred torch, though."

"Nor there is, a very good point. On the actual day, of course, we'll have the real thing, belching hell-fire and Drumfechan flame. To-day we shall content ourselves with some imitation faggot. You have a knife?"

"In my sporran pocket," Charlie said.

"Go then, and cut something suitable down the bank. There's a good chap, we shall await you here."

Charlie went to carry out instructions. "So far so good," said the Laird of Drumfechan. "How could it be otherwise on such a day?" He sniffed the air, turning to savour the beauties of the day, and that was when the Laird invoked his Deity.

Along the Green Avenue from the Big House direction came a bicycle, and riding the bicycle was as bonny a lassie as man could wish to see. Her hair would be, perhaps, the colour of the birch leaf in the dying year. Her skin was blessed by sun to be, perhaps, the colour of the beech leaf in the dying year. And it was summer now. And Margaret Oliphant was spring, in a summer dress with flowers for spring, the daffodil, the tulip and the crocus, a simple inexpensive thing to clothe a treasure. And Maggie smiled, at one with nature's beauty, humming, humming—the "Eriskay Love Lilt," she was humming.

"A miracle every time I see that gel," the old Laird muttered. "Damned awkward miracle at the moment."

She took one delightful leg from pedal and put foot to ground and said good afternoon and smiled, her smile another kindly blessing.

"I thought you were down at Shanwell, Maggie," said the Minister.

"I was," she said, "to meet the staff, and they were just as nice as they could be, especially the Director, a very intelligent understanding man. I told him what you had said, Mr. MacTaggart, about the effects our controlled Thermo-Nuclear Reaction might ultimately have on the lot of the common working man. . . ."

"Margaret, m'dear gel, always fascinatin' to hear you talk." The Laird was puffing out his cheeks, darting anxious glances over his shoulder. "And I don't want to hurry you, but . . ."

Maggie seemed not to hear the Laird. ". . . And he was most interested. He said the question of automation caused him grave concern, because success in our field would inevitably lead to that. Well, to make a long story short, Mr. MacTaggart, he asked me, as a sort of self-indoctrinating holiday task, to undertake a rural study in depth, and I am very much hoping, with your opinions and experience to guide me, Mr. MacTaggart, to prepare a paper for my new Director entitled: *Automation and the Highland Gamekeeper.* . . ."

But Maggie turned. She turned from getting her own back on Geordie MacTaggart in an earnest half smiling deadpan way, and instantly her face changed —jaw set, eyes glittering, the lips a thin red line, the nostrils flaring. "Well, if it isn't wee Charlie Jock," she said in a cold dead voice of hate, and rode away along the Green Avenue to Drumfechan Village without another word.

"*Wha's yon?*" It was a croak, a strangled question in broad native speech.

"Yon is Margaret Oliphant," said the Laird. "Now let's get on with it. Step to the milestone, Charles."

But Charlie had growled, and he was gone. He was running, he was floating, he was flying with that extraordinary stride along the Green Avenue towards Drumfechan Village. Charlie bore his imitation faggot, a stout stick cut from the sapling ash, much the size of a policeman's truncheon.

"Would it be bodily harm that he intends?" said the Minister. "Och, my goodness, surely not."

"I don't know. I really don't. Come on, George! Quick, man! Drive us!"

The Minister squeezed in the back. Urged on by the Laird beside him, Geordie drove at a good thirty along the Green Avenue. Bicycle and torch-bearer were no longer in sight.

"Now we shall have violence, even murder—and I am accessory, I sent him for the murder weapon. Faster, George!"

"I canna go faster," Geordie said. "And the Laird should keep calm."

"Calm! How can I keep calm when I see that killer streak in action? The MacTaggarts, God knows I ought to know them. That lovely gel, her cranium broken and bloody in some ditch, and all my fault."

The remaining ditches were deserted, as was the Square, but that lovely girl had propped her bicycle against the Roman Brig, and she leaned over the parapet in a haunting curve of legs and sit-upon and back, and behind her stood Charlie, weighing the faggot in his hand.

"Stop, Charles!" screamed the Laird.

"Ssssh!" Geordie said. "Look at him."

There was no violent intent in Charlie's face. The Laird let out a long breath of relief. "Stop the engine, George!"

"Please, Maggie, can you not turn round?"

"I'm busy. I'm looking for salmon."

"Och, to hell with salmon. Maggie, please!"

Maggie turned her head, but not the rest of her. She looked him up and down with frank dislike. "What's the stick for? What kind of a show-off is it this time?"

"It's not a show-off, Maggie. It's supposed to be the Drumfechan Torch I'm to carry to the Games. It's one of the Laird's daft notions, Maggie."

"*The Laird's daft notions.* The Laird has more

sense in that wise old head than you'll ever have in your swelled turnip if you live to be a hundred. The Drumfechan Torch, indeed! Who would you ever carry a torch for but yourself?" Now Maggie stood up straight to face him, and she was the taller by perhaps two inches. Six foot of deep-bosomed Maggie to five foot ten of piper-chested Charlie. "*Buzz off*," she said.

Charlie ran on. Maggie turned again to look for salmon, and Geordie squeezed past her back-view with not too much to spare.

"H'mm," said the Laird. "Remarkable. I thought that boy was made of sterner stuff. *Please*, *Maggie! Maggie*, *please*, indeed. But how is it possible that he never knew about Margaret's glorious transformation?"

"The times we ever mentioned her name, he would just stop the conversation flat, or walk out of the house. And he's hardly been home in these five years."

"Yes," the Laird said. "Yes, I see. Well, here we are." They had reached the field where the Drumfechan Games were held. It had been a redoubt of the Roman Camp, and the old fortifications still showed as even grassy banks. Round the field loped Charlie MacTaggart with little spirit. But he had fulfilled his undertaking, and he handed the faggot to the Laird, his Chieftain.

"I'm sorry, sir," he said politely. "I couldn't quite see my way to doing this at the Games."

"Never mind," said the Laird. "Never mind, m'boy. It was a daft notion, I quite agree. But many thanks. Now let us drive you home."

"I think I'll walk," Charlie said. He looked a bi

forlorn, and walked away, and then he ran again in the direction of the Roman Brig.

"Punch-drunk," said the Laird. "Oh, damn that gel, much as I appreciate her words of praise. *Who would you ever carry a torch for but yourself?* No torches no more. That's well and truly torn it. *By hook or by crook to the winning post.* So much for our proud motto. By what hook, by what crook does one get a love-lorn loon to race? One doesn't is the answer." The Laird tugged his wide moustaches in despair. "Ah, perfidy, thy name is woman. I give up."

The Minister coughed. "If a certain perfidy could be persuaded for the honour of the glen to be always riding a certain bicycle in a direction of withdrawal, would a certain love-lorn loon give chase?"

The Laird doubled up, smacked his bony knees, one-two. "As I have said so many times, and must now in all piety repeat: we have only God to thank for the clergy. But how to prevail upon that gel? Let us not forget that the soul and memory of Maggie Elephant reside in Margaret Oliphant. I don't despair, but our problem is well-nigh insoluble, I fear."

"Ticklish," said the Minister. "*Only God to thank for the clergy.*" He giggled to himself in the back of the car across the Roman Brig and the deserted Square and to the Manse where they left him, giggling.

★ 6 ★

Here, Bridget was fast asleep upstairs. Here, Geordie and Jean were talking in bed. Somewhere away outside, Charlie played a slow march, making Highland music in the dusk. The sound of the pipes was growing and fading. "He's a grand piper," Geordie said.

"He's a grand boy every way."

"It was good him telling us about the plane to-night, and earning the money for it with his stories, and how he hopes to use it in his work."

"Aye, I'm glad he told us. I'd like fine to read those stories, Geordie. It's just like him not to bring any of them in the Yankee magazines, not wanting to show off. Whoever says Charlie MacTaggart is stuck-up can watch out for me. He doesn't put on airs. He doesn't think he's any different from what we are—just plain folk in a cottage. I ken the stuck-up one—yon Maggie Oliphant."

"Och, Maggie's no' stuck-up. Maggie's decent. You were saying so yersel."

"Well, I was wrong. Here's Charlie doing his very best to patch things up. And what does she do? She treats him like dirrt and rides away on yon bicycle. And which of them is the most to blame? Which is the one who gave him away to his dad that time he was in trouble? I ken what yon lassie needs, and that's a real good skelping. And if I was Charlie, that's what I would give her."

"If you were Charlie, it might be you who'd get the skelping, Jeannie."

But Jean did not laugh. "Aye, she's strong, like a muckle horse."

"Like a braw muckle filly, mebbe," Geordie said. "Not just quite a muckle horse."

"You're the Clydesdale, you should know. You're the one the muckle filly's aye been daft about, it's true."

That danger always lurked. "Mebbe it was," Geordie said. "Like a lassie's crush-like. Not now though. Now Maggie just pulls my leg. The Laird and her, they team up on me."

The piping stopped, and began again. Now it was a lament, a sadness of music as the long day ended.

"He's unhappy, Geordie. I hate to see our boy unhappy."

"Aye," Geordie said. "But our boy is learning too."

"She's hard-hearted, though. She started training Charlie because the Laird persuaded her to do it, and it was for the glen and everything, and the Laird could persuade a Communist to be a Tory if he set his daft mind to it. And it was against her will, give the lassie her due. But now she knows he's good, and she wants him to win, and you know why? So she can spite him by saying he did it for his own sake, just for selfishness."

"Och, Jean! Maggie's not like yon."

"Maggie's just like yon. I know. I'm a woman too. Now Maggie Elephant has got him round her

M

little finger, where he has to be so she can hurt him. And you know what'll happen at the end of this summer when he goes to his job in Vancouver Island? It'll be good-bye, not just for now and again but always —shut away us and Bridget and everyone and everything—all his unhappy memories of home. And he'll make a grand success, far beyond just being a forestry engineer. He'll smother the goodness that is in him, and train the hard man that is in him too. Our Charlie will succeed. It's as certain as anything could be."

"But life's been too easy for him," Geordie said. "As we were saying, and the Laird was saying too, failing a few times could do Charlie a world of good. Wouldn't it be good for him if a lassie led him a dance and turned him down? Isn't that what he's been needing?"

"Yes," Jean said. "But not for spite to harden his heart." She reached over. "Geordie!"

"Aye, Jean?"

"There's you in Charlie, but there's an awful lot of me."

"I know," he said. "The brains and the punch and the grand hot heid."

"Geordie!"

"Aye, Jean?"

"I'm glad it was you. Every day always I'm glad it was you."

Now the brief summer night had come, and now the sad music had gone except in memory. Soon Geordie and Jean were sleeping.

She was waiting at the hill gate. She had her bike. His trainer always had her bike. On wet days she wore a plastic waterproof. On cold days she wore a sweater and her kilt. On hot days she wore dark-grey Bermuda shorts and a blouse of some bright colour. But almost all the month it had been hot, each day her skin a little browner, each day her hair bleached fairer by the sun, each day her body and her face more beautiful. "Hallo, Maggie," he said.

"Hallo," she said. "This morning I want you to run up to the boathouse, start slowly on the steep bit, work it up to three-quarter speed. Now two things especially always: your breathing and your stride. When you get there, breathe five minutes, hands on hips and totally relaxed, I said *totally*. Then down at half speed until you meet me, and we'll take it full clip up again. Got that?"

"Got that," he said.

"And when you reach there, stuff this piece of paper in that keyhole."

"Why stuff this piece of paper in that keyhole?"

"So I'll know you haven't cheated like the last time. Off you go."

He put the paper in his sporran pocket and he started up the hill. She was very strict with him. You had to do exactly what the trainer ordered. If you did not put this piece of paper in that keyhole, she would say, not angrily but coolly: *If you can't do what I ask, then do it by yourself.* Good-bye for that day.

Soon Charlie was going strongly. *Your breathing and your stride*, working for them, slaving for them, a slave to them. Until this month I never was a slave to anything, he thought.

If you want to run fast, you must run far, she said at the beginning, some forgotten time or other. *How do you know all this?* he said, because she really did know. *Oh well, at one time* . . . But she said no more. Was that how she did it? Did she run the terrible fat off her? But he did not dare to ask. He groaned at the memory of his unkindness, at what a cruel little beast he used to be. He knew that Maggie had not forgiven him, and perhaps she never would. Why should she?

And she was right about the running—twenty, twenty-five, thirty miles and more a day, until every muscle, tendon, ligament was through the stiffness and the soreness and the bind, to be in tune with running, to be made for running, the natural gait— and the same thing with his lungs.

She made him run on grass such as the parks or the Green Avenue, or on the road, pacing him on her bike. But she never let him run free across the hill, the way he had run when he was a boy. *Too risky*, she said. *Turn your ankle, and you've had it.* And she watched him like a hawk for strain and sprain.

Now, at the end of the month his body was a running machine, no more, no less. His mind, such as remained to him, had one image only, one lovely disapproving image. Even her back view on the bicycle was strangely disapproving.

He was near the old gravel-pit when he met his father, or his father was crossing the road and waited for him. "Well, Charlie boy," he said, and would have liked a talk, but Charlie was in the inviolable rhythm of his orders.

"Hi, Dad," he said, and Geordie MacTaggart smiled. He had a grand rocky face to crease with kindness. He was everything in his nature that Charlie would like to be and could not be.

Charlie, Dad said last night with that diffidence of his. *What does running matter? You're not having a holiday at all.*

Don't worry, Dad, he said. *I like it now.* He knew that his father and his mother and the old Laird, too, were in cahoots of worry. He was not worried himself. For the first time his life was wholly simple. He had one golden object, and he ran after that.

He swung left beyond the quarry, and along the boathouse track. The west wind made a small riffle on the loch, a mile and a half long by a quarter wide, in a trough between the hills. The outlet ran from the farther end down into Altnadean. Charlie reached the wooden boathouse, and stuffed this piece of paper into that keyhole. Then he put his hands on his hips and faced the wind and breathed, totally relaxed. *I said totally.* It was true that your body could become the by-all and the end-all. It was damned ridiculous, and it was true.

The five minutes as nearly up as not to matter, he ran at half speed to meet his trainer, and she led him, silently as usual, at full clip to the loch again. "That was good," she said. "Good," she said about the proof of his integrity—she had signed her initials on the paper. "Here's your jersey," she said. "Put it on and jog along the loch and back, and keep to the sheep path. I think I'll fish a while."

"It's hot, though," he said. "I don't need the jersey, Maggie." She sighed, and so he put it on, and went off jogging. He had run ten miles this morning, most of it fast uphill. By this time jogging was to Charlie what a quiet stroll would be to a man in the possession of his senses. He knew quite well that he was brainwashed crazy round the bend, and he did not give one little damn.

He jogged all the way to the end of the loch, and started back. But the sheep path jigged or jogged out of his trainer's view, so Charlie stopped jogging. He went to search among the bell-heather, which was just in bloom. And then he jogged back to the boathouse. She had four small trout, taken in shallow water out beyond the reeds. But Maggie was having a bit of difficulty with those reeds.

There was another rod on the boathouse rack, so Charlie started fishing too. Soon he had six, but two of them were tiddlers, and he put them back.

"Och, damn!" she screamed, caught up in reeds again.

"Could you not pick up your flies a wee bit sooner?" he suggested.

"Could you not for once stop telling people what to do?"

He had not for one whole month, so far as he could remember anything, told anybody what to do. But Maggie was vexed. So he said nothing, and soon they both laid down their rods, and he put the trout in sphagnum moss, and then they sat.

They would sometimes talk in these times between the running—about the countries where they had been, about her kind of work and his, about the corruption that was destroying political democracy. All impersonal talk. But if he ever asked a thing about her own life in these last years, she would clam up. *Many parties down New Zealand way?* he dared once to ask. *Och, parties! That's all you ever think about.* Like every personal thing she said, it was very unfair and slightly true. After four months in the bush, what was it that you thought about if you were human? I used to be human enough, he thought. I may have been an SOB, but dammit I was human.

"Maggie," he said now, the wavelets lapping at his feet. Would she say it was a party boy's daft superstition? "For you," he said, and thrust it in her hand.

"White heather!" she said. "And not just that, but white *bell* heather, madly lucky. Oh, thank you very much." She looked down at his rare discovery, smiling, actually smiling to herself. "I'll put it in my brooch." So Maggie threaded the sprig of heather through her plain silver brooch, and very bonny it looked against her pale red blouse, and she patted it, quite pleased, and smiled again, and caught her breath.

"I hadn't told you," she said briskly. "But it's the day after to-morrow that the selectors come."

"Selectors! What selectors? What are they in aid of?"

"They're in aid of the Olympics," Maggie said. "Surely even you know that."

"Oh," he said. "I'd slightly forgotten."

Now she was vexed with him, which happened unaccountably and rather often. "*Slightly forgotten.* Don't you know that's why I'm training you? And if it wasn't for the Laird's persuading me, I wouldn't, no by God I wouldn't."

"Okay," he said. "I quite see that. But how can they select me when I've never run a race?"

"You're going to run a race, and on the Green Avenue, just as you've been doing." Maggie paused.

"Not against anyone, but paced by me." She stared
at him. Her brown eyes could be soft, he knew, but
not when regarding him. She did not tell him much
about his progress. All she said a few days ago was
You're crowding four. "And I want your best for them,"
she said quietly now. "*Flat out!* Do you know who
they are? They're the very same men who selected
your father for the shot-putt twenty-eight years ago."

"The very same," he said. "How very very cute."

"And what have you to be so cynical about? Isn't
it an honour? Isn't your father ten times the man
you'll ever be."

"How right you are," he said. But she took that
for cynicism too, picked up her rod, and went to the
boathouse. Charlie followed. Chaps say they're all
the same, he thought, not with cynicism, but in
wonderment that his desire for her should be so
physical, so pure indeed, so painful and so hopeless and so humble. And the nearest thing to a
kindly word that he had had in all this month was
just now when he gave her a piece of white bell
heather.

He shuddered, seeing for one dreadful moment the
sameness of all the other ones fly by—the nice ones
and the bitchy ones, the cheery ones and the neurotic
ones, and a jolly decent bag or two, and one and all
they shed a tear for him. Recumbent shadows, ghosts
forgotten.

He laid his rod beside Maggie's in the rack, and
locked the door and hid the key, and he followed her
out again to stand behind her as she looked across the
loch. She wore one of those blouses that come half-
way off the shoulders, and she sighed, perhaps about

the burden of this task that she had undertaken for the Laird's sake and the honour of the glen.

He was half mad after the month of tortured training, and he saw that soft brown skin move to her sigh, and Charlie went altogether mad. He put his hands on Maggie's silken shoulders and turned his cheek to lay it on her neck, and she did nothing, and he smelled her hair, and she did nothing, and he touched his lips to the sweet soft trembling valley of her neck, and she did nothing.

But then his hands were grasped, and she did something, and he flew over her head to lie on deep old heather, it was not a painful fall.

"Look!" she said. "Just look! The first white bell heather I ever had, and you destroy it!"

Yes, all the white blossom had been torn from the heather sprig, perhaps by his fingers in the shock of somersault.

"I'm sorry, Maggie," he said. "I'm very sorry."

"Bah! What were you ever sorry for? Now follow me!"

She led him on her bicycle. It was a terrible dance downhill she led him.

* 7 *

"Doom, George, gloom!"

What reason would there be for feeling doom and gloom? It was another day of grand weather. And once again the Olympic Selectors had come to Drumfechan. They were the same men too—Harley, whom Geordie had not known well; and Rawlins, with whom he had shared a cabin across the Atlantic. They had become good pals in the time they were together, but it was twenty years since Geordie had had a last Christmas card from old Bill Rawlins.

And here he was again. *You're just the same—You haven't changed a bit yourself.* And about the essence that might be true. But the same men had changed at the hand of life.

"Bloody old fool," the Laird said morosely. He shook himself, shaking off the doom and gloom. "Come now, Polyanna, be the life and soul." The Laird stalked away in his droopy kilt to talk to Charlie and soon he had a brief smile on Charlie's face.

Harley and Rawlins were talking with Maggie about how they would time the run, and whether the milestones had been checked for accuracy, and asking this and that about Charlie's training, and they were watching him. They looked at Charlie with the casual dispassion of a pair of buyers at the Newmarket Sales, or the Perth Sales, or whatever. "The physique's all

ight," said Harley. "He's a bit fine-drawn for my
aste," Rawlins said. They were not here as a favour
or the sake of Auld Lang Syne, but because once
before a Presbyterian minister had written out of the
blue from the back of beyond, telling the result of the
shot-putt at an obscure Highland Games. But this
was quite a different proposition, no evidence of
achievement, nothing but the same minister's diffident
word that you might be making a mistake if you did
not have a look. They were amiable men, sceptical
out of an immense experience. "What's his best
time?" asked Rawlins. "Not just too bad," said
Maggie blandly. "We seem to have been here before,
Bill," Harley said, and they shattered the peace of
the glen with laughter. It was quite surprising,
laughter not being of the mood.

"Nice chaps," said the Minister. "I'm not sure,
though—I'm not sure it wouldn't be a better thing
if Charlie didn't manage . . ." He left the rest of it
unsaid.

"Yes," Geordie said. "I was thinking that too."

"It's a far cry from the other time, from your time,
Geordie. Those were simpler days."

"Aye," Geordie said. Simpler days—and happier
days, the Minister might be meaning.

"How long has he been training?" Rawlins asked.

"Four weeks," she said. "That's all his training."

"All his training, period? His *total* training?"

"Yes," she said. "It's been quite intensive."

"Quite," said Harley.

"Quite," said Rawlins. "*All* day, every day?"

Maggie nodded.

"No relaxation?"

"I wouldn't know," she said. "I believe he plays his bagpipes in the evening. Apart from that I wouldn't know."

I wouldn't know. I wouldn't care. Harley and Rawlins frowned, not bothering to hide their disapproval of a trainer who wouldn't know. A beautiful trainer, which was something new. A beautiful cold fish, but that was nothing new.

The Laird and Charlie had walked the other way towards Drumfechan. Now they walked back; and without any warning, the Laird bellowed: "What the hell are we waiting for?"

Everyone jumped except his friend Charlie, who said: "Good point."

Harley and Rawlins had walkie-talkies, which they checked again. Then Harley and the Laird and the Minister got into the selectors' car and drove along the Green Avenue. Charlie took off his kilt. "I'll put it in the Mini, Dad," he said. He was leggy in his running shorts and vest. He was long legs, deep chest. *A running machine*, he said last night. *That's me*, and went to play the pipes. Where was the vital bad-boy Charlie?

"All ready at this end, Bill. How do you read me? Over."

"Loud and clear. How do you read me?"

"Same."

"Okay. When you're ready, then," he said to Charlie, ignoring Maggie Oliphant, who sat on her bike beyond the milestone, one foot to the ground, the Minister's stop-watch in her hand.

Charlie jogged a little, watching her. There was no wind at all this afternoon.

"Flat-out," she said.

"Yes, Maggie. I'm ready when you give the word."

"*I'll* give the word," Bill Rawlins said. "I shall say: Get on your marks, Get set, Go. How do you read me, Tom?"

The voice came over. "Still read you loud and clear."

"Okay," Rawlins said. "Get on your marks . . . Get set . . . Go."

And Charles was off, pursuing Maggie Oliphant.

They followed in the Mini. "Good enough action," Bill Rawlins said.

There was a stick at the two-furlong post. Geordie had set them to show the small intermediate marks. "Quarter coming up," he said.

"About sixty-one seconds," was all Rawlins said.

"About sixty-two," he said at the half-way mark. "H'mm, she shouldn't be pacing him, though." But now Maggie drew far ahead.

"About sixty-one," Rawlins said at three-quarters of a mile, and the others were in view along there by the milestone. "Good God!" he said. "Like a bloody sprinter." And Geordie remembered the other time, the happy time, the simple time—he remembered as clearly as if it had been yesterday, Rawlins saying, or was it Harley: *Good God Almighty* when they watched him put the shot.

"Close!" Rawlins said. "Close as you can." And Geordie drew close beside Charlie's flying heels, beside the spikes that rose horizontal, upside down at each thrusting, driving stride. And then Charlie's mile was over.

"What did you make it?" Rawlins said.

"Four minutes five and a fifth. You?"

"Four minutes five. Are you sure about the measure ments?"

"I told you," Maggie said. "Mr. MacTaggart an the Minister checked it with a tape." She looked her own stop-watch, nodded and clicked it back t nothing.

"We made it a mile and two feet one way," said th Minister, "and a mile and one foot six the other. No just perfect." He giggled, and was silent.

"And on grass," Bill Rawlins said. He looked the grass, which was cropped close by sheep. "Non too short at that," he said, kicking the grass. Messr Harley and Rawlins looked somewhat bewildered and they walked off together.

Charlie jogged the other way and back. He wa sweating, but his breathing had almost fallen back t normal. Maggie sat on the bank beside the Gree Avenue. She plucked a daisy and put it in her mout and chewed the stalk.

"Was that all right, Maggie?"

She nodded, the daisy bobbing in her mouth, an she took it out and said: "Yes, fine." A faint smil a frown, and put the daisy back and looked at th grass. Geordie looked down at the River Fechan, an so did the Minister beside him. And the Laird watche a cock chaffinch singing on a branch. Charlie wer to the Mini for his kilt. Not counting the selector who were in earnest confabulation along the way, ther were five people here, and none spoke now until th Laird said: "Cheerful chaffinch, anyway," and adde loudly: "What are those fellas gassing on about?"

Which had the desired effect, and they came back

Charlie," Bill Rawlins said, and he spoke carefully. He was about sixty now, and heavy in the girth, but till a sturdy man. "Given first that the distance is ccurate, and allowing for grass and a track that isn't lead flat all the way, we would estimate your time— vhat might be called your compensated time—to be hree fifty-seven or a little better. In which case it is y two seconds the fastest mile that has been run in Britain this year."

"A stout effort," Harley said. "It's really quite phenomenal. I mean, congratulations."

"It was Maggie," Charlie said. "Not me." He ooked at Maggie, but she did not stir.

"So there would almost certainly be a place for you f you could reproduce to-day's form or even near it, at he White City Meet next week-end."

"You mean a *race*?"

"Yes," Rawlins said. "And a race in this context means a competition. Even your father had once won n public before he was selected. Right, Geordie?"

"Right," Geordie said.

"To choose you blind would put us and you and veryone in a hopelessly awkward position, even if ur decision were to be endorsed by the committee, vhich I doubt."

"Sorry," Charlie said. "No dice. I'll run in the Olympics if I'm wanted. I said I would, and so I vill. Otherwise, nothing doing." He looked quite mused, quite like Charlie MacTaggart for a moment.

"That settles it then," said the Laird of Drum-echan. "You say you want him to run a preliminary ace, and I see your point, indeed I do. Charles says :'s not in the contract, and I'm with you, my dear

boy, a thousand per cent. So an impasse. Very simpl
You can't select him."

"Don't misunderstand us," Harley said, with a
anxious look at Rawlins.

"You're quite positive about it?" Rawlins said.

"I told you. Sounds arrogant, I know. But I didn
ask to run a mile. So you decide. Now I'm going
change." He looked at Maggie. "No more?" he sai
"No more to-day, Maggie?"

She shook her head, raising her eyes not quite
his, and Charlie jogged for home.

"He didn't ask to run a mile," said the Lair
"You heard him say so. In short, Charles does n
want to run. A waste of time, he thinks, and I hearti
concur. No good selecting a reluctant horse, no
is it?"

"But he *does* want to run," said Maggie Olipha
taking out her daisy.

"Oh, damnation," said the Laird. "I'm goir
home." But he remembered hospitality. "Won
you come in for a drink before you leave?"

They would like to do that very much. But tw
things first. One, they really must check the distan
with the 500-foot tape they had in the car, no questio
of doubting, but you know, more than their liv
were worth if any mistake. Two, they would ve
much like to talk to Miss Oliphant about trainir
methods.

The Laird strode off, and the Minister rode awa
not at all his cheerful self; and soon Geordie dro
the Mini back to the Big House, where the Lair
awaited him.

"I'm bothered, George," he said. "And not on

bothered, but I blame myself entirely, which makes botherment far worse."

"I'm just as much to blame, sir," Geordie said. "I always wanted Charlie to run. And even Jean, she wanted it too. And Maggie's right: Charlie himself does want to run now."

"Why, George?"

"Because that's what Maggie wants. Jean says she wants it out of spite."

"Possible," said the Laird. "I never did understand the female mind, and nor do the women, damn their souls. But she has the boy hypnotised; that vital young fella is like a besotted monkey on a stick. This hardness in Margaret—I don't like. In fact I dislike it very much."

"It's kind of inhuman," Geordie said.

"Can't we stop the whole blasted thing at the eleventh hour?"

"No, sir," Geordie said. "The moment they gave way about him not having to run a race beforehand— that settled it."

"Can't you speak to Margaret, George? I tried to, and she simply said she was doing what I asked her to do because I asked her, and for the honour of the glen. The honour of the glen, my foot. That will teach me to indulge in second-rate facetiousness. She wouldn't discuss it further, clammed up on me. Couldn't you try her, George?"

"I have, sir, twice. And I got nowhere. The first time she made rings around me with her brains, and daft jokes about automated keepers and my shaky hand and all the rest of it. The second time she just walked away."

N

"Yes," the Laird said. "You certainly cooled of that mammoth crush in no time flat, a brilliant effort and much to your credit, George, because despite these unfortunate traits which now reveal themselves in Margaret's character, she is, I will admit, a young woman of extraordinary appeal to anything male from the cradle to the wheel-chair. Hence poor Charles' predicament. This coldness, though—if you had the strength to pin her, George, I would gladly beat the wench."

"Jean would gladly murder her," Geordie said. "Jean says that Maggie Oliphant is doing her best to make sure that Charlie never sets foot again in Drumfechan."

"I know," said the Laird. "That's the ghastly thing, and all my fault. Please accept my apologies, George, for the little that they're worth." The Laird did not wait for Geordie to say anything, but went up the steps at an old man's pace.

Messrs. Harley and Rawlins drove down the glen. They were warmed by the Laird's good whisky, and Geordie's Hogmanay bottle too, but low in their own spirits. "If he flops we're going to look a proper pair of suckers."

"Oh well, perhaps they won't agree to it."

"Of course they'll agree to it. We haven't got anyone else within three seconds of Bonham—or Larsen—or Sunotek. MacTaggart's the absolute only hope."

"I'm none too happy about him, though. On the one hand, a tensed-up racehorse—and what a racehorse. On the other, an infatuated yes-man to the gorgeous gorgon. No real spirit to him—not like Geordie. Old Geordie was terrific."

"Still is. Still the monumental rock of ages. Funny, isn't it, that in all our thirty-five odd years at it, the only blind choices we ever made have been from one family in one outlandish glen. I suppose that's why I've always remembered Geordie."

"Yes, twice unique. The Laird and that clergyman and Geordie himself—it could be yesterday, with decrepitude added. Except in one thing—they're all as worried as hell. What about?"

"About that female obviously. Young, and a smashing dish to look at, and when I offered her a free trip to Montreal, Quebec, Olympic Games as private coach—and what a fabulous coach—how could she bulldoze him into it in four weeks? How? —I offer her the trip, a chance that any girl on holiday—and she is, all summer—would jump at, and what does she say? She says: *No.* Not, no thank you very much. Plain *NO!*"

"There is one thing that might explain it. Do you remember afterwards when we were making conversation with the Oliphant, and I said: *Geordie has hardly changed except for a few grey hairs, wonderfully young for his age*, and her face lit up, and I thought: My God, perhaps she *is* human after all, and she said: *Yes, Mr. MacTaggart's young-looking, isn't he, and much younger in himself than he likes other people to think.*"

"Well, what about it?"

"I'll tell you what about it—she's madly in love with father, who gives her the brush-off. So what does she do—she gets her own back on the son who's madly in love with *her*."

"How does training him in a period so short as to be miraculous—training him to be the best miler we've had since Bannister—how is that getting her own back?"

"Because, idiot, she doesn't give one little damn about him winning races—she's got him in her pocket —faithful Fido plodding after her for weary miles, day in, day out until she's broken him. Notice how old Moustaches kept talking on to us about Charlie —*splendid boy—a brilliant academic record, y'know— witty chap—a bit hard-driven these days, not quite himself.*"

"But Geordie wouldn't have any truck. That Jean is a damned attractive woman still, and they're obviously dotty about one another."

"Of course Geordie wouldn't. But don't forget the ancient saw: *Hell hath no fury* . . . And what better way for a jealous female to get her own back?"

They drove on.

"The same lovely place. Peace, perfect peace. I thought of that other time, with all their little favourite squabbles about nothing, about which hawk takes the chickens. Remember?"

"Yes. And Geordie declining to put the shot for *England.*"

"But to-day no squabbles, not a one."

★ 8 ★

"Good-bye, then. I hope you win."

"Do you?"

"Why would I have trained you all this time if I didn't hope you'd win?"

"You trained me so you could get your hooks in me, so you could wrap me round your little finger. Oh yes, you wanted me to win. And you know why: for spite."

"Who said that?"

"*I* said that. I'm saying it now. Spite, spite, that's all that's in you. Spite when you told on me to Dad. Spite to get rid of me and make me hate my home. Spite so Maggie Elephant could have revenge. Spite so that you could say I won for my sake."

"You never did anything in all your life except for your sake."

"Well, now I'm going to. I *am* going to win. And do you know why? I'm going to win to spite you."

"That would still be for your own sake. Hateful wee man, not even worth hating. The same dirty slimy Charlie Jock."

Margaret Oliphant walked home slowly, and more slowly, with her bicycle; and Charles Ian MacTaggart walked with his pipes to the Piper's Cottage to play a few last tunes above the sombre Piper's Pool

It was to be good-bye to-morrow morning, and London for Charlie to fly over with the team. He wa leaving three weeks earlier because of the Olympic Games, and he would not be back. *Well, I get a fre ride out of it*, he said, laconic and subdued.

"Is he still playing?" Jean called now from bed.

Geordie opened the back door to listen. A late blackbird sang nearby, and down there, a mile o more away, the pipes were playing still. He wen upstairs to see that Bridget was tucked-up all right and to see her innocence asleep, and a kiss for hi child and down again. The pipes had stopped.

"I'm feared for him, Geordie, there alone, and him so sad, and the terrible old piper's tale."

"Not now," Geordie said. "It would be after, would worry."

"And what can we do after, when he's gone? And he'll not be back, he as good as said it."

"No, he'll not be back."

"So that's both our sons we lost."

Geordie took her hand. What was there to say?

"That's nice," Jean said. And in a while she said "I got him alone to-day and I sat him down at the kitchen table and I told him a few things about Miss Margaret Oliphant."

"You shouldn't have done yon, Jean."

"Mebbe I shouldn't, but I did. It's bad enough to have him turned against his home. That's done. Bu it's worse to have him pining for a wicked lassie."

Which could be so. Perhaps his passionate Jean was right. "Jeannie!"

"Aye, Geordie?"

"We'll give him a cheery send-off in the morning."

"Head up, chest out and shoulders square. Och aye, I'll do my duty."

"It's no' the chest that worries me."

"Geordie!"

They heard Charlie come in and go upstairs, and the hollow clunk of his bagpipes as he set them in their case.

"All the five years he had his pipes with him to keep home with him, so he said. But this time he's leaving the pipes behind."

Their boy came downstairs again to brush his teeth. Then the window was opened above their own. "It's true," Charlie said to himself up there. "*For my sake. It is true, isn't it?*"

They were in the smoking-room, and the Laird's big television set was on. Bridget was drinking ginger beer, up late by special dispensation. Geordie's mother and Jean sipped sherry. The Minister nursed a modest deoch an' doris. Geordie had a man-sized dram. The whisky decanter was convenient for the Laird's own noggins. It was nearly eight o'clock, and the screen still had a tuning diagram of lines and circles. "There's something wrong with that invention of the devil."

"It's not time yet, sir," Geordie said.

"Margaret's parents had to go to Perth, but she promised she would come. Where is the gel?"

"And now world-wide and live by television satellite from the Olympic Stadium in Montreal, here is our

NBS commentator, Richard Martin.   But first we
pause for station identification . . ."

Maggie Oliphant came in.   "Oh, Margaret.   Just
in time.   What will you have to drink?   A glass of
sherry, or there's . . ."

"Might I have whisky, please?"

"Of course, of course."   There was a faint stir from
the ladies who sipped sherry.   Geordie's mother
occupied a chair with wooden arms.   She sat in ample
dignity.   *Queen Mum Salote*, the Laird called Mum
behind her back.   *Queen Mum Salote takes a dim view
of me this morning, George.   I spurned her kipper.*

"No, thanks, Mr. MacTaggart, you stay there.   I'll
be fine by Bridget."   Maggie sat on a footstool with
her legs curled round, and she took a long swig of her
drink.

"See if you can get it better, George.   Too pale.
Too pale."   The Laird was fidgety.

Geordie did some tuning.   "How can I see with your
vast bulk in the way?"

Geordie moved aside, and went on tuning.   "That's
as good as I can get it, sir."

"Leave it, then.   Leave it, many thanks."

Geordie knew how the Laird was feeling because
he felt like that himself, and Jean was tense, and
Bridget was excited, and Geordie's mother leaned a
little forward.   Only Maggie's face showed absolutely
nothing, her whisky half-way down already.   She was
thinner, a little pinched about the nostrils, but her
face showed nothing.

"Good morning, good afternoon, good evening,
ladies and gentlemen and boys and girls all around the
world.   Hallo, everyone.   I am Richard Martin, and

it is my especial privilege to describe to you the high-light, the greatest event of all in these great Olympic Games—the final of the fifteen hundred metres. The weather is perfect here in Montreal, about eighty-four degrees, and not a breath of wind, and the stadium is packed, jammed full of humanity to the very rafters. The runners will be out in just a moment. A privilege for me. Yes, if I may venture one personal note, an especial privilege, as I shall tell you later."

"Tell us now, you fool," said the Laird of Drum-fechan. Richard Martin did look rather foolish, all grins and excitement, but he made you feel the excite-ment too.

"Ah, here they are." The camera switched to a few men on the track, this side of a fuzz of faces. And Geordie remembered, how well he remembered that inhuman hugeness of humanity in an Olympic Stadium. "We'll take them by the numbers that they've drawn. First, Number One, Mark Bonham of Australia, world record holder at this distance and the mile, slender build, deceptive, almost ethereal, but just you wait and see. Bonham is strong favourite . . ."

"There's Charlie Boy," Bridget screamed. "He's Number Three."

"S'ssht, Bridget."

"Number Two is Sunotek of Hungary . . ."

But Geordie did not listen. He watched Charlie jog while the voice went on about Sunotek. The picture varied a little, but always sharp enough to know that that was Charlie.

"Number Three is Charlie MacTaggart, and by a strange coincidence, here's my personal note, forgive me. Twenty-eight years ago I was a cub reporter on the *Boston Globe*, and I saw a young man lift a car that had pinned a poor guy underneath; and I wrote the story, and that young man was Geordie MacTaggart who the next day won the Olympic shot-putt.

"*And Charlie is his son!* Yes, Charlie is the great Geordie's boy. Perhaps it was Geordie who made me choose the sports desk soon after, and I've been covering sports ever since, this way and that. Geordie was the dark horse then, and Charlie is the dark horse now, an unknown runner until he won his Olympic heats, not in spectacular times, but don't forget he *won* them. To say he's good is to state the obvious. Good enough to take Bonham? I simply do not know.

"And just as big blond Geordie was a favourite with the crowd, so is slim dark Charlie. He's a bit withdrawn. He's totally electric. Hardly bothers to notice the girls, but boy! Do they notice him! So that's Charlie MacTaggart, Britain's white hope, the black-headed Scotsman. *How's your dad?* I said to him to-day. *Dad's fine*, he said with that magical quick smile. Hi, then, Geordie, wherever you are away up the glen! Think of it, father and son! Ah, there's blood in these MacTaggarts."

"You're telling me," said the Laird, and the others laughed, and Maggie smiled a little. "Remember your admirer, George?"

"Dicky Martin," said Geordie. "Yes. I've hardly thought of him from that day to this." There had been a picture too, that included wee Dicky Martin between Geordie and Helga Sorensen, the lady shot-putter, but Geordie had been careful not to bring that home.

Dicky Martin, now called Richard, talked about the other finalists. He talked a bit too much, but he was good. The long and the short of it was Bonham a hot favourite, Larsen of Norway to be reckoned with, MacTaggart the unknown quantity to watch.

"It's any second now. They're off! Sunotek out in front—Larsen—Bonham—MacTaggart—all going well."

The picture was getting weaker. Strange world, strange world indeed that you could watch your son running over in Canada, and you would grumble that the picture was not sharp enough, and the Laird was cursing. "Can't you make it better, George?"

"No," he said, and the Laird was quiet.

"First lap done. Now Sunotek's falling back. Now Larsen widens the gap from Bonham. No, Bonham's holding, and MacTaggart's holding Bonham. It looks like a race between these three."

The picture was fading altogether. "Please come back," Jean said. "Och, please."

But it did not come back. "Second lap over. Still Larsen, Bonham, MacTaggart. The rest are out of it, I think. Yes, too far back in this company. They're out of it. No change with the leaders. Who looks strongest? They all look strong. Larsen the big Norwegian with the cross-arm action, not pretty but it works for him. Bonham, his arms rather wide, his body upright, lean as a greyhound, those pistons pump. MacTaggart, deep-chested, a wonderful natural action, that . . .

"Coming round now. Coming into the final lap."

And the picture came back bright and clear.

"Now Bonham's challenging, and MacTaggart is

behind him, right in behind him. They're catching Larsen. They've got him, Larsen falling back. Oh, what a race! I tell you, never have I seen—Bonham has it, Bonham has it. Wait, though! Coming into the finishing straight, three feet between them. They're sprinting like tigers. Now MACTAGGART's coming, yes, he's coming, Charlie's coming, fifty yards to go . . ."

Not a stir in this room, not a movement, but Maggie muttering, Maggie muttering. "No, it's Bonham, it's Bonham, MacTaggart can't quite make it, game as the devil but he can't quite make it, smiling, yes smiling as he finishes a yard behind. What supermen these fellows are. What true sportsmen . . ."

Now Maggie burst out sobbing and she ran away.

"Oh dear," said the Minister. Such hopes . . . Oh dear.

"Disappointing," said the Laird. "But what a splendid race. Wonderful, wonderful." Mumble, mumble, and the Laird was frowning.

They watched until Bonham's time was announced —three thirty-five and one-tenth—a new Olympic and World Record, and MacTaggart beat the old record too. And then they watched the medals being presented, the Gold for Bonham, the Silver for Mac-Taggart, and the Bronze for Larsen. "The boy looks happy," said the Laird. "He does. He really does look happy again." And there were Charlie and the Governor-General of Canada laughing together as he got his medal.

So that was that, and time for Bridget to go to bed. "Margaret all right, George, do you think?"

"Disappointed, sir," said Geordie; and he frowned and thanked the Laird and bade the Laird good night.

"Greeting because he didn't win!" Jean said, and her look was as black as Jean's black look could be.

"But, Mum! Maggie was saying: *Don't win, Charlie. Don't win, Charlie,* a million times in the last round. She was right beside me, and I heard her."

"For spite, then," said Jean.

"What's spite?"

"Bad thoughts," Jean said. She was past caring what she said about Maggie Oliphant in front of Bridget.

Bridget stopped on the path beside the monkey-puzzle. And she shook her head. "No, Mum," she said in firm rebuke. "It wasn't bad thoughts. It was good thoughts Maggie was saying to Charlie."

"*Don't win.* How can that be good thoughts?"

"It was, Mum. *Please don't, Charlie,* she said near the end. Is that bad thoughts, the way Maggie said it?"

"Come away then, Miss MacTaggart," Geordie said, and he swung her to his shoulder.

It was nearly dinner-time next day when Geordie met Alec Oliphant in the rain.

"Wha's daein', Geordie?"

"Nothin' special, Alec. Wha's daein' wi' you?"

"Nothin' special, Geordie. I hear tell your laddie put up a grand performance in them Olympics in yon race."

"Aye, Alec. It was thanks to the training your lassie giv' 'im."

"Oor Maggie's terrible put-out. She was greetin' in her bed a' nicht."

"She would be sair disappointit that oor Chairlie didna' just quite win."

"It was hersel' she was currsin', 'n a terrible currs is oor Maggie."

"Hersel' she was currsin'. Is tha' a faact?"

"Aye, tha's a faact. And the door is lockit, and th wife's greetin' too the noo, and soon it'll be Olipha that's greetin'. When the wummen start greetin', fair turrns ma stummick."

"Me too, Alec."

"Geordie!"

"Aye, Alec?"

"Mebbe if it was you spoke to Maggie, she woul stop the sobbin'. Just wild, it is. It's a lot for to as Geordie, but we're worrit desperate, and her still at a' the forenoon too."

"Well, Alec, mebbe I could try, if you'd come to for company like. A wumman greetin' just fair turrr ma stummick."

"Me too, Geordie."

They went into the shepherd's house, and up th stairs and to a closed door. "I'm the most disgustin horrible beastly bitch. I always was and . . ."

"Maggie!"

A sob, no answer.

"It's Geordie MacTaggart."

"Och, go away, you boring big galumph." Mor sobs.

Geordie went away.

"Geordie!"

"Aye, Alec?"

"What's *galumph*?"

"I dinna ken. Not just too polite like by the sound eh, Alec?"

"Not just too, I'm thinkin', Geordie. Sorry, Geordie."

"Och, they're a' the same when they get dementit. What's to do, though, Alec?"

"Search me, Geordie."

"Would you mebbe get the doctor to her, Alec? Too much greetin' can be like the hiccoughs, even fatal."

"Aye, and for the doctor to be hurrled oot the windae—yon can be fatal too. Ye ken wha' Ah'm thinkin', Geordie?"

"Let's hae it, Alec."

"Ah'm thinkin' oor Maggie's been richt queer these past six weeks. Ah'm thinkin' a richt guid skelp is what oor Maggie's needin' for a doctor. Wha's to dae it, Geordie, though? She's a muckle lump o' lassie for to skelp."

"Aye, she's a muckle lump o' lassie for to skelp. I've just the yin idea, Alec, like a last resort."

"Tell us, then, Geordie."

"When I'm passin' the Big Hoose the noo, would I mebbe tell the Laird?"

"Aye, do yon, Geordie, ta."

Geordie posed the problem while the Laird stared out of his window. "H'mm," he said. "It takes a self-styled Magus to be a proper bloody fool."

"What was that, sir?"

"Oh, nothing, George. Okay then—I shall cope with the young lady after luncheon."

"How, sir, if it's not a rude question?"

"The question is not rude, and the answer is a piece of cake. First I shall apply the tongue-lash, brutal, unadorned. Then I shall soften up with

butter. Then I shall scourge with cruel whips—meta
phorical, of course. Elementary, my dear Watson, a
the great sleuth remarked to the torpid leech. *Adios*
George."

But the Laird hastened to the telephone. "Mar
vellous," he said to himself while waiting briefly. Th
Laird's attitude towards modern invention was, t
say the least, ambivalent.

". . . Oh, you did? Well, have a Horse's Neck
Have three. There's nothing like them. Now lister
here . . .

". . . You have to *what*? See your new Japanese
friend again? Explain." Then the Laird had a
choking fit. "Hang on," he said, choking. Choke
over, he said a little wanly: "I shall need some warning, though—at least three hours. Take care, old
boy. *Festina lente!*"

* 9 *

It was two days later that the Laird again went to cope with Margaret Oliphant. She came to the back door of her parents' house. She wore dirty sneakers, bluejeans, a sack-like sweater. Her hair was a mess, her expression hostile. The Laird catalogued the young lady's appearance from top to toe and up again.

"Well?" she said, not quite the way for the shepherd's daughter to welcome the Laird.

"Margaret," he said mildly. "You know my great-niece, Mary—the one who's had mono-nucleosis."

"Yes," she said. "A nasty drawn-out thing, it is."

"But on the mend now, I'm glad to say. Well anyway, I had a note from her mother this morning, saying that Mary's appetite has just begun to come back, and you know how choosy invalids are, particularly children." Margaret nodded. All true so far; now careful: "One thing Mary keeps asking for, one thing only. *Mummy*, she says, *if I could just have a trout or two or three from the hill loch at Drumfechan, the wee ones, Mummy, that taste so delicious.*"

"Och, the poor bairn," Margaret said, her brown eyes soft. They were remarkable lambent eyes.

"So the thing is, m'dear gel, I thought I would try to catch some, put them in ice and on the London train to-night. Unfortunately, though, one of these forestry commission nincompoops is coming to see me at two o'clock. So I can't fish myself. Could you possibly take the Mini and do it for me? It would do Mary so much good, I know."

She hesitated. "I'm leaving for Shanwell to-morrow morning."

"So soon, Margaret?"

"Soon! What's there to do in this dim place?" said Miss Oliphant, her eyes less soft. But thought of the child came into them again. "Perhaps I could manage an hour or two this afternoon."

"Oh, would you? What a kind gel you are. At two then. And if you're back by fourish, that will leave plenty of time to put them on the train. Half a dozen should be quite enough."

"Half a dozen might be too many. I'm no good at catching those quick wee trout."

"The quick wee man catches the quick brown trout," said the Laird, and checked his traitor tongue by a smart change of subject. "Look, Margaret," he said. "It is none of my business, but since it has been my privilege to know and admire you from infancy, it is certainly also my ancient privilege to draw attention to your appearance. The clothes I do not mind so much, but that unkempt hair—you might be a Shakespearian witch of tender years."

Margaret blushed hotly. "Who cares?" she said.

"*I* care. And what will this forestry chap think of us? What will he think at four o'clock if the most beautiful Junoesque damsel in all Scotland comes in looking like the spaniel's dinner? So buckle to, my good woman, take a pull."

The Laird made his escape. A mettled wench, he thought. Lucky fella who brings that to heel and to bed and to cook his breakfast.

He dropped off height, flying in from the west, not hedge-hopping because there were no hedges to hop, but hill-hopping—up to three thousand and more than that, down to two thousand and less than that, fooling the radar net, he was a bit light-headed, flying since time began or some time or other.

And here it was—small car, small building, small boat, small loch between the hills. One little mile or so of hill-hopping to celebrate, touch wood about so many endless miles of luck. Now careful.

He examined the loch at a safe and sober altitude. He knew the shallows and the rocks as well as one might know them waterborne, but that was not quite well enough. Satisfied, he came in for his landing from the east, change pitch, full flap. The boat had moved in against the shore.

Almost, almost, rip, rip-rip to meet and rush and roar and sink and slacken, and it was done. He gave her throttle to taxi up the loch. He asked the engine to work just once again, faithful engine all the way to home. "Thanks, Old Engine," Charlie said.

He took off shoes and socks, rolled up his trousers and went paddling in the peaty water—one line from float to rock, one line from the other float to jetty, and she was secure.

Then he lay down, heather for his bed, heather for his pillow. Am I? he thought. Did I? Could I? Montreal to Seven Islands, Seven Islands to Goose Bay, and then the pack ice, white circles of it, how could white circles fit together? But they did, off Greenland's icy mountains to an iceless place called Iceland, then at last a place called Scotland, and the customs and the customs and the customs, and one telephone call, and sleep, three hours of sleep among people's legs in a waiting-room, a teaspoon of the bucketsful of sleep he needed, and one ham sandwich and a cup of coffee, and here we are, not really here. And what does *really* mean?

He looked along the loch. The boat seemed nearer. "Honey bee," he said. "Buzz, honey bee." He went to sleep, not deeply, he was still too tired for that, skimming, skipping from the fifteen hundred metres to the Greenland ice, hopping a last hill to home, and that noise was oars being shipped, this noise a boat being dragged ashore, and this noise footsteps on the sand. But keep your eyes shut. Shut your eyes.

"Maggie!"

"Yes, Charlie?"

"Just checking." He went to sleep again. This time he was following that bike, up hill, down dale and round the bend, that goddam bike.

"Och, goddam!" she screamed.

He sat up to watch. The heather hills swam round a bit, and then they steadied, and he watched Maggie casting.

He got to his feet and walked along. "You're not quick enough," he said. "Here, I'll show you how to do it."

She gave him the rod, and he showed her how. After the third trout, he said: "Nothing to it if you're really good. Now try again."

Maggie did as she was told, missed one, missed another, got one.

"Funny thing. I dreamed I was following you on that bike, that goddam bike was what I dreamed just before, I'm sure it was before your imprecation. Psychic, really."

Her eyes flickered, and she went on casting. "Whose aeroplane is that?"

"Mine," he said. "My very own."

"Where did you come from in it?"

"From Canada, of course."

"How long have you been flying?"

"For ever," he said. "I can't remember ever not. How long have you been fishing?"

"An hour or two," she said. "I can't remember. The Laird wanted some trout to send down to that Mary, the one who's been so sick in London."

"Oh yes, I see."

"How did you get the plane?"

"I'll explain some time."

"Got you!" It was a good one for the loch, almost half a pound.

"The heather is bonny now it's all in bloom."

"Yes," she said.

"And the water is bonny in the sun."

"Yes," she said.

"And the wild cotton in the bog is bonny."

"Yes," she said.

"Is it only being so tired that makes the world seem new and beautiful to me to-day?"

"Why don't you sleep again?"

"I think I might go jogging first. Would it be all right with you if I went jogging?"

But she did not answer.

Charlie went jogging to his faithful plane, and put on shoes and went off jogging.

"Hey!"

"Yes."

"Are you hungry?"

"Vastly." And he went off jogging along the loch.

The smell of fried trout met him coming back. It was a double boathouse—one half for boat, one half for rudimentary kitchen. She was humming a tune in there, an old familiar tune with words of Charlie, and she stopped. Out here he hummed a tune, an old familiar tune with words of Maggie, and he stopped. "Present for you," he said.

Maggie Oliphant came out. "Oh, you found some more. How could you find two bits of white bell heather?"

"The same," he said. "The same rare plant."

"I'll put it in my brooch."

"We must be more careful of good luck this time."

"Yes, Charlie, Charlie Boy. I love the way Bridget calls you Charlie Boy. Am I allowed to?"

"Yes. But what about those trout?"

"They should be just ready now."

"Share them with me."

"No," she said. "You flew a million miles for them. Now eat them, and then you'll have to catch some more for Mary."

Charlie ate the trout, all six. Now sleep swooped in upon the heels of hunger.

"You won't go away?"

"No," she said. "I'll be your pillow. I just chanced

to be fishing. Now I can just chance to be your pillow."

He lay down in the heather, and she was his pillow. "Why did you come back?"

"Sleeping," he said, and so he was. He slept for ever, flew for ever, ran for ever, and flew again in the drumming plane above circles of the Greenland ice. One yard about, and Bonham—One yard, and Bonham—Two feet, and Bonham. *Don't win, Charlie. Don't win, Charlie. Please don't win.*

"Charlie!"

"Why do you keep on waking me?"

"You've been asleep for ages. *What* was that you said just now?"

"Dunno. I was dreaming that I heard your voice again."

"Again? Did you hear it in the race?"

"Yes," he said. *"Don't win, Charlie. Please don't win.* Not in my ears exactly, in the middle of my head."

"Was that why you came back?"

"Of course," he said.

"But why the awful endless journey in that little plane?"

"I'm me," he said. "You're you. Please don't win for my sake, your sake, our sake. Fair enough?"

"The announcer said you smiled just before the end, and I thought I saw it too. Would you have won?"

"I don't think so. One more foot I might have gained. Mark Bonham is too good." His head was in her lap, and she was crying. "Don't cry, Maggie."

"I was so awful to you all those weeks; trapped worse every day, riding—riding, running—running, until it became the only thing—to *make* you win. Not for spite, though, Charlie."

"I know," he said. "We were both dragged round the bend."

"That day here at the boathouse. I knew by then that you wanted to win yourself. And I knew by then how good you were. And when you came up behind me, I thought: *At last. Now we can escape it.* And so we could have, but you would never have run another step, and I would have cheated you. Didn't you know when I stood so still and then you kissed my neck—— Didn't you know?"

"I knew I was on the ground. How come you learned that trick?"

"There was a boy in New Zealand who taught me a little Judo once."

"There was a chap in Canada who taught me a little Judo once. He was the gold medallist, turned out to be not too bad a teacher. In fact he threw Mark Bonham and me quite painlessly all over every joint in Montreal. And then we practised on the other customers—could hardly lose with this Japanese chap to lend a hand when necessary. Then we each took an arm and tried to give him a lesson in running away from cops. That worked less well. But the cops were very kind and drove us home. So that's how I learned Judo. Got the point, my little one?"

"Yes, Charlie Boy. I love you more than any woman ever loved wee man before."

"That's good," he said. "And no sooner was I dropping off to sleep at seven a.m. after a long hard day and night of it with Bonham—what a menace— than the Laird of Drumfechan telephoned."

"*The Laird telephoned?*"

"Yes, to say that things had reached a pretty pass —that you had just called the man you revered most in all the world a *boring big galumph*, and would I in the circs consider coming home? And he also reported that Bridget heard you saying what I heard you say myself. So that was a telepathic shock, and here I am at the appointed place and time."

"And all this fishing was a put-up job?"

"Just a put-up Laird job, trying to keep his chessmen happy."

"Let's go down and see him, shall we?"

"Yes."

"Two manly tears," she said. "I thought only silly Maggie Elephants were prone to tears."

"He's been so damned good to me all my life."

So in due course they went to see the Laird.

Farewell

It was a grand marriage in the Scottish sense, with all the people of Drumfechan at the Kirk, and other old friends too. Alec Oliphant gave away his daughter, and Bridget was the only bridesmaid; and the best man was Tam Burrell with whom Charlie more than once had been in trouble.

So the Minister joined them as man and wife. Sometimes, if the bridegroom were to be shorter than the bride, you might think it not quite natural or right, or even a wee joke. But nobody thought a joke about Charlie and Maggie. He was two inches smaller, Maggie's man; and she was two inches taller, Charlie's woman, and that was that, black-headed Charlie and his bride. What love could be more true than love that found itself through trouble? What truth could be so bonny?

The Laird had insisted on giving the reception, a saving for Alec Oliphant, and a pleasure for the Laird, Charlie and Maggie being in a way the lively children he had never had. So champagne was passed round, and the Laird made a speech proposing Maggie's health. He said little, and the jokes were not his very best. After that the cake, and Charlie's reply for Maggie.

The bride went to change from her wedding dress, but they were not to start on their honeymoon from there. They were to fly from the hill loch, not all the way to Canada, though. *Both headwinds and the wee wifie would tend to pose a fuel problem*, Charlie said. So they were going to have a flying honeymoon, and then ship the plane somehow. When Geordie said: *Where will you find the money?* Charlie just answered: *Time will tell, Dad*. It was a new world certainly, gamekeepers' sons with aeroplanes, and shepherds' daughters, bright hopes of the scientific world who said: *I couldn't care less about controlling the Thermo-nuclear Reaction*.

Everyone got into cars and drove up to the loch to see them off. It had been a nice cool day, with the wind in the east, which meant a chance of mist as evening came. So they said their farewells quickly— as farewells should be said—and taxied away, down the loch and back again to warm the engine up. Now turning, waving, and now off.

"Godspeed," the old Laird said. The Minister's lips were moving. It rode higher, higher, would it ever rise? But the plane was off and swung back this way and dipped its wings good-bye again.

Geordie drove the Humber limousine, the Laird and Jean and Bridget sat in the back in real dignity. The other cars had gone before.

"I'll be Auntie Bridget soon."

"Yes, Bridget," said the Laird. "You will."

The hill gate was open, and Geordie stopped beyond to close it.

"I think I'll get out here, George. Mooch about a bit."

"The mist's nearly down, sir," Geordie said. The Laird looked tired, he thought.

"Do you imply that I am incapable of blundering down to my own house in my own Scotch mist?"

"No, sir," Geordie said. "I mean you need your cape."

"Ah, fusspot. Pshaw! Well, good night, you three MacTaggarts."

They said good night to him, and he stumped off in his best kilt, as droopy as his ragged one, towards the trout-hole, into which Jean once fell. But, not for the first time in history, the Laird had a second thought.

"George!"

"Yessir?"

"Just what the boy needed to make a man of him, a bit of trouble, eh, George?"

"That's right," Geordie said.

"George!"

"Yessir?" No doubt a third thought coming.

"Lang may yer lum reek."

"Same to you, sir," Geordie said.

"It's usually *lums*," Jean said. "Eh, Geordie?"

"Aye," he said. It usually was, unless the Laird of Drumfechan happened to be reminding his keeper and stalker of a small cave where he had taken shelter with his future daughter-in-law.

"The Laird wasn't daft a bit, and now he's being daft again."

"The Laird's no more daft than you are," said Geordie sternly, as had been said in the Mac-Taggart family for some time now, but how much longer?

"The Laird sometimes says daft-sounding things to cover up he's feeling just a wee bit sad."

"Who wouldn't be feeling just a wee bit sad with Charlie Boy and Maggie gone away?"

"That's right, Bridget."

"I've a mind to walk home, Geordie. Let's do that. Then you could bring the Laird's cape up, and drive the Humber."

Jean had been quiet with a mother's thoughts all day, of then and now and joy and sorrow and good-bye my son. "Come away, then," Geordie said.

They each took one of Bridget's hands, and the three of them walked down together. The mist had come, the quiet mist to shroud a world. But they knew the rolling of the hill. They saw the sweep of it with no ending.